HIDDEN RAPTURE

At first Vivienne was very reluctant to go
to Tangier pretending to be somebody else.
She didn't want to hurt Robert Colby,
whom she was going to be deceiving—
although she wasn't in the least concerned
about his disapproving brother Trent. But
after all the thought of perhaps finding her
lost love Gary again decided her to go
through with it. She had never considered
what Gary's reaction might be if he met
her again . . .

Books you will enjoy
by ROUMELIA LANE

THE BRIGHTEST STAR

Rennie was a mining engineer in South Africa, and a very competent one—but of course she came up against a lot of opposition on account of her sex, and the latest critic in a long line was Todd Dillman. Did her job *really* make her less feminine? Rennie didn't think so—especially when she considered the way she felt about Todd ...

BAMBOO WEDDING

Stranded in Taiwan, Carey had married Brad Hunter purely out of expediency, so it should not have come as a surprise, let alone a shock, to learn that he had married her for equally calculating reasons. Why should the knowledge hurt her so much?

HIMALAYAN MOONLIGHT

Gail was determined to join the expedition into the Himalayas led by Doctor Webb Whitfield—although he didn't want her in the party. She managed to persuade him to change his mind by pretending to be engaged to another member of the party—which rather complicated matters when Gail found herself falling in love with Webb instead!

THE TENANT OF SAN MATEO

Faye was thrilled when she inherited a property in sunny Majorca, but not quite so thrilled when she arrived there to find an unwanted tenant firmly in possession. And there was another condition attached to the bequest which took even more of the gilt off the gingerbread!

HIDDEN RAPTURE

BY

ROUMELIA LANE

MILLS & BOON LIMITED
17–19 FOLEY STREET
LONDON W1A 1DR

First published 1978
Australian copyright 1978
Philippine copyright 1978
This edition 1978

© Roumelia Lane 1978

ISBN 0 263 72818 8

Set in Linotype Plantin 10 on 10½ pt.

Made and printed in Great Britain by
Richard Clay (The Chaucer Press), Ltd., Bungay, Suffolk

CHAPTER ONE

ONE could easily have heard a hairpin drop among the rows and rows of desks at the Betchfield Mail Order Company. A few minutes later pandemonium broke out as the bell signalled the end of the working day and the female clerks streamed down the corridors to the outdoors. In the hardware section thoughts were turning eagerly towards the leisure hours and conversation blossomed inevitably on the favourite topic. Men!

'Oh, I can't wait to get home tonight!' Sandra Gates, a tall flat-footed girl, nosed her way towards the exit with an agitated giggle. 'I'm going to put on my white cuddly fur stole. Brian's had that look in his eye. I feel sure he's going to produce a ring.'

'Gosh, do you really think he'll propose?' Brenda Wallis, a dreamy-eyed eighteen-year-old, gazed on enviously and admiringly while trying to keep up with the flurry of high-stepping heels.

'Don't you girls go fooling yourselves that there's anything cushy about married life,' Betty Sherman, a tired-faced mother of two, put in a little acidly. 'It's twice as hard running a home. You wouldn't catch me rushing into it if I had my time again.'

'That's because you weren't clever about it, Betty,' Hazel Hughes, a bright bachelor girl, spoke up laughingly. 'The trick is not to jump at the first offer but to wait for the right man.'

'And by that she means the one with oodles of noodles,' said Monica Randall, a sharp-faced girl noted for her sly wit.

'That's exactly what I do mean,' Hazel replied sweetly and unashamedly. 'I think the smart thing these days is to measure your man by the luxuries he can provide in marriage, and I bet there isn't an unmarried girl here who doesn't agree with me.'

'Except Vivienne.'

All eyes turned in one direction and someone scoffed goodnaturedly, 'Viv's a dark horse. She never discusses her love life.'

'That's right. I can't say I've ever heard her mention a boy-friend.' Sandra, who talked of nothing else but her male attachments, gazed on, mildly incredulous, and the rest chanted, 'Oh, come on, Viv! Why do you never tell us anything about your romantic life?'

'The answer's really very simple.' Vivienne, holding her own in the jostle of female forms, remarked evenly. 'I haven't got one.'

There were squeals and titters of disbelief which were quickly scotched by Betty Sherman's somewhat pedantic tones. 'I happen to know that she's telling the truth. I've known Vivienne a long time and I've never once seen her with a member of the opposite sex.'

The teasing turned to smiling puzzlement and pity, and Pat Garmes, a spinster on the wrong side of thirty, groaned, 'Cor! Who was that bloke that said youth was wasted on the young? Look at that figure! Makes you go green with envy. And natural waves and all!' She crimped her own spiky thatch and sighed goodhumouredly, 'There's no justice in this world.'

Vivienne kept a calm smile as she always did on these occasions. She didn't consider herself youthful. She was an old and wise twenty-three, and anyone caring to delve deep into her heart would have found the remnants of bitterness and hurt there.

'I'll tell you what, Pat,' someone suggested matily as they came to the dark, damp outdoors. 'We'll go to the local palais some night. They get a nice crowd on Saturdays and you never know your luck.'

'I'll try anything once,' Pat quipped drily, joining in the laughter against herself. There were cheerful goodnights before they were swallowed up in the general surge towards the main gates, some pushing out autocycles, others fortunate enough to run cars, leaving behind the ones on foot who lived locally.

Vivienne was one of those who made her way over the connecting iron bridge which led to the company hostel. Below her a fast-flowing river whipped up white foam against rocks in the darkness. It was fortunate that Betchfields was on the outskirts of town. All around was rolling countryside where one could lose oneself on the lighter evenings and summer weekends. From the metal clang of the bridge she came to the dull tiles of indoors. She didn't mind the hollow ring of her footsteps on the stone stairway, the muffled thrum of the steel banister going all the way up to the fourth floor of the hostel, as she climbed. Long ago she had deliberately chosen these surroundings. Cold and impersonal, they suited her.

On the second floor she was mildly surprised to see a door open along the corridor and in the light there was a slight figure in a dress that seemed too big for her, peeping out. 'Lucy!' She hurried forward. 'I saw you weren't at your desk this afternoon.' And eyeing with concern the blotched little face, 'Are you ill?'

'No, I'm all right.' Miserably the girl bit on the corner of her sodden handkerchief. She lifted her gaze, then the pale eyes with their stubbly sandy lashes were brimming with tears again. 'Oh, Viv, something awful's happened!'

'It can't be that bad!' With an effort at cheerfulness Vivienne gripped her arm. 'Come inside and tell me about it.'

Lucy Miles occupied the room next to hers and they were both about the same age. Lucy came from farming stock. She was inclined to be fumbling and awkward in company and worked at her job as a desk clerk with laborious concentration. Her hands and feet seemed too big for her thin frame and everything she wore looked oddly out of shape. But Vivienne had recognised a shy sincerity and warmth behind the girl's colourless looks and they had become firm friends. She was closer to Lucy than anyone.

Inside the room she led the way to the foot of the bed. The furniture was sparse and had a clinical plainness. A trunk and suitcases filled the space along one bare wall. Now what's wrong?' She hugged the other girl. 'Not trouble at home, is it?'

Vivienne had no close relatives and on occasion she had gone with Lucy to the tumbledown farm dwelling some miles out on the far side of town. She knew the story surrounding the girl's family. Her father had lost his hand in a tractor accident and her mother and two young brothers worked hard to hold the farm together. Lucy, who loved the open air, plodded on with her job at Betchfields to bolster the family income.

'No, everything's fine. I had a letter this morning.' She blinked her gratitude for the thought through tear-filled eyes, slumped and gulped, 'It's the other letter. And all those I've written. And I never told you nothing ... and now ...' the look on her face was like that of a trapped animal and there was a wild light in her tears, something like grief, '... I just don't know what to do ...'

'You're not making much sense, Lucy,' Vivienne said kindly. 'What letters are you talking about? And why should you have told me?'

For a moment it seemed as though no coherent reply would be forthcoming, then with an effort the other girl straightened, dabbed at her eyes and with wan purposefulness began to explain. 'Do you remember that time when we went to the club social and one of the church women there got on to us about spreading a little happiness among those less fortunate than ourselves?'

'Mrs Dermott with her pen pals abroad thing, you mean?' Vivienne reflected smilingly. 'Yes, I remember. It was just before Christmas, wasn't it? About three months back.'

Lucy nodded and in between smoothing the hem of her handkerchief with blunt fingers she said sheepishly, 'I didn't say anything to you, but before we left I got her to give me one of the addresses.'

'I see,' Vivienne said with a knowing gleam, but her friend gave her a look of such agonising sorrow that all attempts at flippancy failed. She picked at her handkerchief.

'His name's Robert Colby. He has a muscular disease and he can only get around in a wheelchair. Mrs Dermott heard about him from some people back from holiday last year and she thought he'd like someone to cheer him up. He's twenty-four. He used to be a rugby player, and he's still got a fine physique ...'

'Lucy,' Vivienne interrupted gently, 'are you telling me that you've been corresponding with ... with Robert ever since that night before Christmas?'

'Every week,' Lucy nodded. 'Sometimes twice a week when the mail allowed it.'

Trying her best to gather what she could, Vivienne remarked, 'Then I take it you've grown rather close?'

'We love each other.' It was not so much a confession as a stark and hollow statement devoid of everything but a desolate and crushing dejection.

Vivienne was at a loss. She gave a puzzled laugh. 'Well, if you feel that way why the ...?'

'Oh, Viv!' Lucy's tears were brimming again. 'You don't understand. Robert's going to die. Here!' She fumbled in the pocket of her dress and tossed out a letter. 'Read it. It came this morning.'

Vivienne smoothed out the folded piece of paper. *Dear Miss Blyth* ... The fact that this was her own name didn't penetrate her consciousness, for she was too absorbed in the terrible message that followed ... *I have the unhappy task of informing you that Robert's condition has deteriorated. There seems no hope. His doctors are not optimistic of him surviving more than a few more weeks. He is asking for you. I would appreciate it if you could travel out here as soon as possible—at my expense, of course.*

Despite the tragedy behind the message the wording of the letter was terse and formal. It was signed *Trent Colby*.

Vivienne looked up. 'Well, at least there's something you

can do.' She tried to sound bright. 'You can go and see him.'

'Don't you see? I can't, I can't!' Lucy thumped the bed and stared at her friend in silent anguish. Then with a sigh she got up and brought something from a drawer. 'This is a picture of Robert. It came with his first letter.'

Vivienne saw the smiling face of a blond young man with a bull-necked kind of ruggedness. 'He's very good-looking,' she commented, laying the photo on the bed between them.

Lucy nodded and stared down at it and then as though casting her mind back to their first introduction by post she said wistfully, 'I've never had a boy-friend.' And with a deprecating smile at herself, 'Well, look at me!' She dabbed her eyes. 'I did so want everything to go well. Robert wrote such a nice letter and I wanted him to like me and——' There was the ripping sound of her handkerchief. 'Oh, Viv! I don't know what possessed me, but I sent him a picture of you!'

'Of me!'

'Yes,' Lucy gulped miserably. 'You remember the one you gave me for Christmas? . . . in the leather frame?'

That one. Yes, Vivienne recalled the likeness. The camera had caught the laughter on her lips but not the shadow behind her smile. She remembered she had written some lighthearted comment in one corner and signed it Vivienne. Though a little confused now she smiled at Lucy, 'Well, that's not the end of the world.'

'But it is! It's the end of Robert's if he finds out. Don't you understand? It's the girl in the photo he's in love with, not me.'

Lucy dabbed furiously at her eyes again and Vivienne was beginning to comprehend. 'You mean you've been writing to Robert all this time under my name?' she said slowly.

'Yes,' Lucy snuffled. 'You never get much mail, only forms and circulars, and I always bring it up for you anyway. I just took Robert's letters addressed to you to my room.'

Vivienne mused. Now when she came to think of it, she had noticed the subtle change in Lucy over these past months—the flushed, elated look on her face sometimes, the quick laughter and happy nervous fidgeting. 'But why?' she implored her friend gently. 'Surely you must have known that that kind of thing wouldn't work.'

'I did.' Lucy looked wretched. 'But I had to write as Vivienne Blyth. Your signature was there. And it was such a lovely photo—Robert said it was in his very next letter. I kept meaning to tell him what I'd done. But we were getting on so well, I didn't want to spoil things. I truly did mean to write the truth to him some time, and now . . .' she began to wail into her balled-up handkerchief, '. . . I never can!'

'Oh, Lucy!' Vivienne put an arm round her. 'You're the kindest, sweetest person I know. I'm sure Robert won't mind when he learns that you're the girl who's been writing to him all this time.'

'We can't tell him now!' Lucy's tones were horror-stricken. 'How could we be so cruel as to destroy all he's built up for himself in his mind when he has only a short time to live? No, Vivienne,' she seemed to have suddenly come to a decision, 'Robert believes that you're the girl who wrote the letters, so there's only one way. You'll have to go to him.'

'I?' Vivienne was thunderstruck. She gave an incredulous laugh. 'That's a perfectly mad idea, Lucy. I could never carry it off.'

'Yes, you could,' her friend said firmly. 'It's only for a little while, remember,' she gulped back a fresh uprush of tears. 'And you'd be doing a kindness for Robert. And for me.'

Vivienne took her friend's hand and held it while she spoke. 'Lucy, I do realise that this is an awful muddle and that it would be unthinkable to confront Robert with the truth now. But don't you see, I haven't a clue as to the relationship between you two. What would I talk about?'

'I've got all our letters.' The blotched little face looked hopeful. 'You know how Miss Otis is always dogging us to keep a copy of everything. Well, I always did that when I wrote to Robert. Besides, it was nice to look back on what I'd said when I received his reply.' Shyness gave way to pleading. 'You could read everything we've written to each other, then you'd know how to behave. I have a month's holiday due to me. You can have it and I'll work in your place. After that I'll get you some kind of extension.' Lucy sat up straight, wearing a crumpled yet decisive air. 'Robert's going to die, Viv. We can't spoil his happiness now. You must go first thing tomorrow to Tangier.'

'Tangier!' The floor seemed to open up in front of Vivienne and she felt as though she was balanced on the edge of a yawning black hole.

'Yes, Robert lives there with his brother. He's very rich. He runs a casino. He has a beautiful villa ...'

Hardly hearing, Vivienne rose and went to stare out of the window, seeing not the dark gleam of the factory fore-court in the lamplight below but a scene of teeming alley-ways and golden beaches, women with veiled faces and natives in djellabas. Tangier! The city she had spent four years trying to forget. Trying to shut out the burning memories of Gary Thornton and the idyllic months they had spent there together before he had calmly said goodbye and cruelly walked out of her life. Young, full of life, crazily in love, his going had sent steel doors crashing down over her heart, never to be opened again to any man.

'I'm afraid the idea's out of the question, Lucy.' She turned from the window pale-lipped. 'I can't possibly go to Tangier.'

'Oh, Viv!' A wailing started up from the bed. 'I was so sure you'd agree to help. I know I did a silly, foolish thing sending your photograph, but how could I have guessed it would end like this?'

Compassion mingling with an abhorrence in her to agree to the plan, Vivienne stared at the bowed head. She was struck by the irony of the situation even in the midst of her unhappiness for her friend. While she had striven to build a life for herself far away from the glamour of foreign places, shutting out all thoughts of romance or contact with the opposite sex, Lucy had been yearning for these things like a flower struggling for the sun. Writing abroad to Robert had filled a pathetic need in her, but the tender relationship which had developed between them was founded on deception and was destined to end in heart-break from the start.

She met the tear-smudged eyes across the bed and in a painful mental struggle she said with almost the same look of pleading, 'You don't know what you're asking, Lucy.'

'I do.' The chin went up. 'If there was any other way I wouldn't beg you to do this for me.'

The silence in the room was crushing. Vivienne thought of the unfortunate young man in Tangier who was waiting hopefully to meet the girl of his dreams. And because Lucy was her friend and she was afraid she would back out if she didn't speak, she said tonelessly, 'Where are the letters?'

Vivienne sat up most of the night reading. She felt like an intruder blundering in on sacred ground as she witnessed the gradual unburdening of two young hearts; an acquaint-anceship which had begun with the shy formalities of get-ting to know one another and deepened into something that was both haunting and touching in its tenderness.

The knowledge that through mere correspondence Robert and Lucy had fallen quietly in love only served to increase Vivienne's misgivings in the matter. Could she make a convincing substitute for the kind and gentle Lucy? Especially when her own heart lay like lead inside her.

She spent the rest of the night tossing in her bed, obsessed with the fear that Robert would see through her the moment he set eyes on her.

In the morning a cable was dispatched to Robert's home in Tangier and by midday Vivienne was on her way to the airport. Lucy had helped her to pack, shouldered the prob-lems concerning her departure and bade her a tearful good-bye, begging to be kept informed of Robert's condition.

The flight was uneventful. It wasn't until they were

touching down at Bouhalf Souahel airport that Vivienne's insides froze and a reluctance to set foot on Moroccan soil was almost too powerful to overcome.

She entered into the bustle and scurry of this gateway to Africa as remote from the shabby, sweating porters, the dark-skinned travellers in tribal costumes, the bowing, scraping Arab luggage touts, the bored Customs officials as if she were crossing a lonely meadow close to Betchfields. The cobalt blue sky, the distant minarets, rose-gold in the afternoon sun, pierced the heavy drapes of her memory with the keenness of a sword thrust. She moved on, blind to the scene. *She didn't want to remember. She wouldn't!*

A slim girl, alone, in a leaf-green suit and neat white blouse, she was the inevitable prey of the shuffling street guides, the hotel canvassers, the transport vendors. And though she paid little attention to these brown-skinned men in dirty robes and woollen skullcaps, to their whines and cries to be allowed to assist, their presence was becoming slightly suffocating, when a sharp order snapped out there in the air terminal and the tiresome, clawing figures fell away from her like yapping dogs called smartly to heel by their owner.

Through the scattering mêlée a stern-faced man approached. 'Miss Blyth? Miss Vivienne Blyth?' Though the tones were rich and deep a sceptical blue gaze flickered over her as though sizing her up with the photograph Lucy had sent.

'That's right,' she nodded just as coolly.

'I'm Trent Colby, Robert's brother.' And making a sign to the tall hawk-faced manservant accompanying him, 'Abdul will take your luggage. The car's waiting outside.' With a hand on her elbow he ushered her past the robed hangers-on, leaving them scraping by the wayside by his very air of icy detachment.

Out in the fading sunlight the early evening scents of mimosa and lemon blossom stirred the pain in her as she was brought to a stop beside a long black limousine. Abdul, in cool grey djellaba and red fez, was there to open the door for them. Mechanically Vivienne slid into the luxuriously upholstered rear compartment. She paid little attention to the man who climbed in after her, knowing only that his bulk in faultless tropical suit seemed considerable on the seat beside her.

When, a few seconds later, they were cruising away from the airport she tried not to look at the countryside, always so stunningly green, when one recalled that this was Africa, but the view, still indelibly printed on her heart, of date palms and tamarisks and houses of reddish mud, re-awakened all the old ache there. In all these four years it was no better. She could never forget.

She realised after some moments that she was being watched, and it came to her with a jolt that she had a part to play. She pulled herself together and sat straight in her seat. For Lucy's sake she must make an effort to see this thing through.

'Rob talks about you all the time,' Trent Colby was appraising her with his cold blue gleam. 'You two have been writing to each other fairly regularly, I believe?'

'Every week,' Vivienne mouthed Lucy's words. 'Since we first got to know each other around Christmas.'

She saw that sceptical pull of his mouth. 'An odd approach to a love affair, isn't it? Pen and paper and sealed with a loving kiss and all that. Especially when the two of you have never met.'

'Kindred spirits need no physical contact, Mr Colby,' she replied tartly. 'Robert and I knew we were meant for each other almost from the start. But you don't have to believe it.'

'That's right, I don't,' he said in clipped tones. And nailing her with his gaze, 'You're here because Rob's asking for you and I'm relying on you to give him the happiness he deserves. Any time you feel like backing out, like calling it a day because you think you've made a mistake, forget it. I won't have Rob hurt, you understand?'

Face to face with the man it was impossible to ignore the underlying force of his personality. He had reached that stage of maturity where he emanated an incisive, masculine air, not just in his sweeping dismissal of the dark-skinned mob which she had witnessed at the air terminal, but in the way his shoulders filled his suit jacket, in the hard lines of his sun-browned face, the lean flexibility of his wrists. His light blue eyes were keen and searching and only faintly veiled as a man will hide his grief.

Vivienne watched him light up a cigarette. She spoke coldly. 'You don't like the idea of my coming here, do you?'

He shrugged. 'I've no faith in sentiments delivered from afar. When I was Rob's age, the idea was to take a girl in your arms, not make love by proxy.'

'It obviously didn't do much to soften you,' she remarked spiritedly.

The suggestion of a grim smile tugged at his mouth. 'I might say the same for you.' He eyed her closely. 'Why this attachment for Robert? You don't look the type to me who'd be satisfied with a pen and paper romance. You've got the look of a girl who knows what life is all about.'

Despite her resolve to keep at a cool distance Vivienne was stirred sufficiently to reply, 'I don't suppose Robert, before his illness, lived exactly the life of a hermit?'

'My kid brother is just twenty-four years old,' came the tightly smiling statement. 'A mere babe when it comes to dealing with the capricious moods of women.'

'But you've taught him all you know.' She wished she could stop sparring with this contemptible man. Not that it did her any good. He sat there with his detestable, male-like impregnability calmly giving her orders. 'If he'd listened to me you wouldn't be here now. But since you are, you'll go through with what you started with Rob and like it.'

She thought of Lucy and of her tears last night and was fired into retorting, 'Hasn't it occurred to you that you could be terribly wrong about your opinion of ... me? Women do fall wholeheartedly in love through correspond-ence, you know—and men too.'

'That, Miss Blyth—or had we better make it Vivienne since you're going to be part of the family——' a sneer mingled with the scepticism in his tones, 'I'm banking on, from your side at any rate.'

Vivienne flung her gaze out of the window, hardly noticing that they were coming into the city. It was obvious that she and Trent Colby were not going to hit it off. Heavily protective towards his ailing brother, he was suspicious and watchful to the point of open dislike for her motives. Well, the feeling was more than mutual, she smiled thinly to herself. She had plenty of bitterness to spare.

From the outside her gaze roamed over the lush interior of the car. Through the blue glass partition Abdul steered with meticulous care through the traffic. On their side there were carpets underfoot and padded arms on the seats for reclining. Trent Colby's suit was of expensive fabric, a fine powder blue. At the wrists paler shirt cuffs were held immaculately in place by gold cuff-links and partly visible was a precision made gold watch. All this she noted with distaste. She had heard how he made a living, and a man who battened on to the rich for his existence she could do without.

The limousine swerved and she saw that they were leaving behind the wide boulevards with their evening shoppers, so like those in any other city, and making for the green outskirts. She caught glimpses of the ochre walls of the Casbah and the old town as they climbed, of the grand mosque and sundry minarets and domes. Views that she had tried to shut out of her mind for so long were now here to taunt her anew.

At her lowered gaze Trent Colby said, a hint of sarcasm in his voice, 'I'd advise you to make the most of the scenery. You won't have much time for sightseeing. Rob's confined to the house and he'll expect you to stay near him.' What he meant was that *he* would expect her to stay near his brother.

Aloof now from his overbearing attitude, she hesitated, feeling that something should be said here on Lucy's behalf. 'I haven't had an opportunity to express my sympathy over Robert's condition ... this sudden fatal illness ...' her condolences sounded banal and insincere. 'Naturally, when I heard I was——'

'Rob knows he has only a short time to live,' her ramblings were cut short testily, perhaps because there was pain here, 'but he's not maudlin about it. He's always been cheerful about his illness and I want things to stay that way. It will be up to you to give him the companionship he needs, bearing in mind that we never talk about his infirmity.'

They were entering the gates of an estate above the city. On raised ground ahead was a Moorish-styled house, opulent with its sparkling white walls and red roof-tops, its tiered archways and winding stairways. 'We call it "Koudia",' Trent Colby told her in his abrupt fashion. 'It means The Hill.' After this sparse bit of information they drove up through plum orchards and orange groves and on to a drive shaded by cedar trees.

Abdul brought the car to a purring standstill on a terrace fronting the house. Marble steps led up to the lower line of archways through which was the main doorway. Inside where the subdued lighting was reflected in the rich dark parquet floor her host informed her with his unfriendly smile, 'Rob goes to bed at six, so you'll have to wait until tomorrow to make his acquaintance. We'll take dinner in an hour.' He watched her as she turned to follow Abdul and her belongings up the curving staircase and added as an afterthought, 'This is strictly a man's household. I could, if you wish, hire a girl maid to help you with your things.'

'It doesn't matter,' she shrugged off his offer. 'I can look after myself.'

'Just as you like.' Once again the sarcasm was faintly detectable in his tones and with a slight inclination of his head in farewell he strode away towards one of the downstairs doorways.

Vivienne's composure was unimpaired as she climbed the stairs. She had already assessed the interior of the house from the glimpses of rich Aubusson carpets and expensive antique furnishings, and what she saw only served to heighten her distaste for its owner.

Along a tiled corridor she was shown into a spacious room which lacked none of the qualities of the downstairs decor. The bed was draped with damask, Moroccan style, the carpet was red, deep-piled and endless. The manservant switched on the light in a russet-tiled bathroom drew the drapes and asked with French intonation, 'Would Mademoiselle care for any further assistance?'

'No, thank you, Abdul. I can manage now.' Despite his forbidding appearance he had a kindly warmth in his dark eyes and the suggestion of a smile on his thin lips, and she smiled back at him as he went out.

The hour passed quickly. By the time she had unpacked, washed off the dust of travel and changed into a pink linen dress it was time to go down to dinner. She had a mild attack of nerves while she was applying a fresh dusting of make-up. Through the mirror she looked into the brown depths of her eyes, only a shade lighter than her dark brown hair, afraid that there might be some tell-tale signs there. But they stared back at her calm and unrevealing, and re-capping the amber lipstick she dropped it into her handbag and went out.

Downstairs it might have been a problem finding her way but for the fact that across from the staircase a rose-lit interior showed a table set with crystal goblets and winking silver. She moved into the room, the lights catching her hair, the paleness of her bare arms. Trent Colby in white dinner jacket was waiting for her. 'Good evening, Vivienne.' He spoke as though they were old acquaintances, though she didn't miss the slight curl to his smile. 'I hope you found everything to your liking in your room?'

'I'd be exceptionally hard to please if I had any complaints,' she replied evenly.

The chairs were high-backed and intricately carved. He held one away from the table for her and slid it into position as she sat down. In a deadened kind of way she found herself aware of the woody fragrance of his after-shave lotion.

They ate from silver dishes brought in at intervals by a

flamboyant figure in striped waistcoat and balloon-like
trousers referred to as Momeen. Throughout the meal
Trent Colby kept up a suave conversation which Vivienne
could well have done without.

'I believe Rob used to write to you in a little town called
Aylehurst near Oxford. I know it vaguely.' He forked
more meat on to his plate. 'Have you always lived there?'

Vivienne shook her head. 'It's not my home town. I
moved there some years ago.'

'With your family?'

'No. I happened to like the surroundings, so I got a job
there.'

'From what I've seen of the place passing through,' he
said with his dubious smile, 'it seems hardly capable of supporting itself, let alone offering employment.'

'It does, though,' Vivienne replied lightly, with similar
cool. 'There's a huge mail order company on the outskirts.
I'm a desk clerk there.'

'A small fish in a big outfit.' His glance was openly roving. 'You don't look the type to be satisfied with that?'

'Nevertheless it's true.' She went on eating with apparent
unconcern. 'I'm just a working girl.' Then with an upward
tilt of her hazel gaze, 'I'm sorry if this is a disappointment
to you, for Robert's sake.'

'Hardly.' He leaned back in his chair with a humourless
slant to his mouth. 'It's more or less what I expected.'

After the dessert, a light and frothy soufflé, he said,
'You'll find plenty to do around the house. Rob spends
most of his time in the pool—he's still able to move pretty
powerfully in the water. You'll be a disappointment to him
if you can't keep up.'

She lowered her coffee cup uncertainly. 'I can swim
quite well, but ... I thought ...'

'Get rid of the idea that Rob is a sickly invalid. His
kind of complaint allows him to indulge in all the activities
enjoyed by other full-blooded young males.'

Vivienne felt her cheeks flame momentarily and, quick to
notice this, Trent Colby added with his hostile charm,

'What's wrong? Getting cold feet at the thought of physical contact with a boy you've never met?'

Recovering herself almost immediately, she answered with hardly a tremor in her tones, 'I'm sure I'll find Robert as attractive in person as I do in his letters.'

She felt herself being surveyed through a screen of smoke. That blue gaze narrowed slightly as the man across from her drawled, 'The interesting thing will be to see his reaction to you.'

This was dangerous ground, and Vivienne rose unhurriedly and wandered to look at the view from the windows. This semi-interview with Trent Colby was gruelling enough. But the worst was yet to come. What would Robert think of her? Would he see through her?

Fear feathering her nerves, she stood slender and smooth-haired gazing out into the night. There were the shrouded rooftops of the Casbah to tug at her heartstrings again, slim minarets pencilling up into the fluorescent blue of the star-bright sky. Trent Colby came to stand at her side. Musing with her over the scene of the sprawling city and the Grand Mosque bathed in greenish-white light, he offered her a cigarette with the query, 'Reckon you're going to enjoy your stay in Tangier?'

She declined, saying with a doleful smile, 'This is hardly a holiday visit, is it?'

He shrugged his smooth-clad shoulders. 'You tell me?' She didn't miss the bantering steel in his eyes.

She remarked levelly, 'I'm here because Robert needs me. What reasons would I have for travelling all this way other than love?'

'Plenty.' He took a thoughtful pull on his cigarette and blew out through clamped white teeth. 'A chance to live it up in exotic surroundings, maybe. The urge to sample life in a rich Moorish household and have everything laid on for a while.'

So that was it! That was at the root of his veiled sarcasm and smiling suspicions! He thought she was a girl out for a good time, grasping at the opportunity to leave a humdrum job and using Robert as an excuse. Poor Lucy! Poor, dear Lucy!

With ice-cold anger she responded with withering calm, 'Don't mislead yourself into thinking that any of this impresses me.' She made a gesture at the elaborate furnishings at the floodlit mosaic terraces beyond the windows. 'This kind of wealth has a taint to it that I have no wish to be associated with.'

His smile was unaffected. 'So you've heard that I run a casino?' He thrust a hand into the pocket of his impeccable black trousers and that bantering knife-edge gleam still focussed on her as he queried, 'I take it you don't approve?'

'I'm not sufficiently interested to care one way or the other.' She lifted her chin. 'But I hardly think you're in a position to preach to me about what's right for your brother.'

'Meaning that I'm not being fair to Rob?' The quizzical steel in his eyes became a little molten. Then he relaxed his frame and stubbing out his cigarette in a nearby ashtray spoke with lazy familiarity. 'You're way behind the times Vivienne. Gambling is a respectable profession these days, indulged in by royalty and wealthy members of society.'

'Is that why you chose it?' She marvelled at her own nerve confronting this man who could if he wished have crushed her by the mere indolent force of his personality.

'Could be.' Surprisingly he ignored her jibe. There was only the hint of smiling antagonism mingling with his hard expression. He glanced at his watch. 'And talking of work, it's time I was on my way.' Turning to go, he waved a hand towards the rest of the house. 'Amuse yourself any way you like. There's books in the library and music— pop records and the heavier stuff.'

'Thank you, but it's been a long day,' she said primly. 'I think I'll go to my room.'

'I should if I were you.' Somehow she knew he meant to have the last word. 'You've got a big day ahead of you tomorrow. Rob's waiting to meet you and nothing must happen to disappoint him.' He left her with a curt, 'Good-night, Vivienne,' and went out.

Later, hearing his car drive away as she turned down the bed in her room, that hollow feeling of fear took possession of her again. Here she was in a strange household in Tangier taking another girl's part in an affair that was both tragic and dangerous. Had she been wise in allowing Lucy to talk her into it? She had agreed, mainly to shield Robert from the truth, but she had reckoned without the ruthlessly protective presence of his guardian standing by like a leopard watching over a wounded cub. She listened to the fading sound of the car engine and found that her heart was beating fast. Trent would have no mercy on anyone who inflicted pain on his brother. She would have to watch her step with him.

CHAPTER TWO

HER dreams were tortured and when she awoke Vivienne knew why. The first thing that assailed her nostrils was the old familiar scents of the city; spices and sandalwood, kebab, courtyard jasmine and dust-blown streets. She rose heavily thinking how much easier it had been to assuage her unhappiness under the cool, remote skies of England. Coming back was like whipping the dressing from her partly healed heart, leaving it raw and inflamed with memories.

The view when she drew the curtains was like a death blow to it. The sea, a shimmering well-remembered blue, lay flat into the distance, dotted with moth-like craft near the harbour. The Casbah, framed against the tips of dark cypresses, the ragged greenery of eucalyptus, tumbled down the hillside, a complex of ugliness and beauty as its box-type dwellings, its flaking pastel-tinted façades were caught by the lilac and rose of early morning. To her right the white tall-storied buildings and hotels of Tangier, bordered by a golden beach, were almost hidden from view by immense palm groves. And yet down there somewhere was the Boulevard Pasteur and the hotel El Riadh. Would she ever forget its name, or that night when she had first met Gary?

Her fingers clenched round the curtains. She closed her eyes as though shutting out the view would shut out the too-sweet recollections. What had she done, that she should be put through this torment?

The feeling of desolation was short-lived; she saw to that. She had had four years in which to train herself and it was with squared shoulders and firmness of step that she went to bathe and dress.

In a belted striped dress and simple straw sandals she smoothed her hair at the crown to the neat froth of waves at the nape of her neck, allowing it to spring up at her

24

brow, and picking up a straw handbag containing a fresh handkerchief and odds and ends she made for the open glass doorway of her room.

The wide balcony was shaded by a line of archways similar to those on the ground floor. On either side of her were the twin white towers comprising the main rooms of the house. Those standing back under the archways seemed to be given over to guest apartments, but through a doorway across in the far tower she discovered interiors much the same as those she had seen last night. The decor was dominantly French of the Versailles style but with a strong masculine flavour noticeable in the heavy filigree Moorish lamps, stout carved chests and colourful leather accessories. All of it, one could see at a glance, was of the kind to be found only in the very richest of households.

Her smile curled knowingly at the thought as she turned back to the outdoors. The air on the balcony was limpid and soft. There was an outside stairway at the far end, just beyond her room, which took her down to the terrace where the car had pulled up last night. There was no sign of it now, so one assumed that there were garages elsewhere.

Separating the terrace from the main grounds to one side was a line of squat palms and flowering shrubs. It was from beyond these that Vivienne caught the sound of voices and guessing that the swimming pool was in that direction her heart began to knock aganst her ribs. Robert was there; she knew it, waiting excitedly for her to make her entrance, and she had no idea where she was going to find the courage to do so. Suddenly the whole scheme to try and pass herself off as the writer of the letters seemed fantastically wild and crazy. How had she ever expected to get away with it? She toyed with the idea of searching out Trent Colby, confessing that she was an impostor, then making a quick departure. But rooting her there was the picture of Lucy's sad little tear-blotched face, and another one she had conjured up in her mind of a young man sitting in a wheelchair eager to make the most of a small happiness before his time ran out. She gulped back the dry tears and an angry helplessness. It was no good; she was in this thing and there was just no way out of it.

Steadying herself, she went past the palms and following the sound of the voices down a step to another terrace where tall greenery, beautiful trailing plants and shrubs encompassed a magnificent azure pool. There were figures there, a servant perhaps and ... yes, a wheelchair. A pulse began to throb in her throat. Such an incredible distance to walk! And no introductions. She wondered crossly if Trent had planned it this way.

Her sandals whispered over the colourful mosaic surround. She walked with a natural grace, feeling the warm sun on her bare head and, curiously, no self-consciousness at all. She watched the seated figure in the wheelchair draw ever nearer, and then she was there, smiling and plunging painlessly into the part she had agreed to play.

'Viv! You've come at last!' Her hands clasped in a surprisingly firm grip she looked into a pair of eyes a darker boyish blue than Trent's but unnervingly similar. 'Robert! I've waited a long time to meet you.' It was odd but she really meant the words.

After the first ardent hand-clasp they drew away shyly. To give herself time to scrape together more lighthearted remarks she studied the young man in swimming trunks with a gleam of what she hoped looked like whimsical affection. He was very brown, but his thick thighs and muscular arms and shoulders had a pitted look as though crumbling from within. Her throat constricted, but the smile never left her eyes or her lips. Only inwardly did she cry out aloud at the cruelty of fate.

His hair was very blond and thick and straight and framed his square features, much like Trent's but without the jagged corners, in a way that was heart-catchingly handsome. Of course while Vivienne was playing for time he was soaking up the sight of her, a look of wonder and contentment on his face.

'Your hair is just like it is in the photograph.' He reached out and let the silken strands filter through his fingers. And with a quick deep laugh, 'It's funny, but you're exactly as I imagined you, pretty as anything.'

Vivienne slid him an openly admiring look and replied laughingly, 'I'm not going to inflate your ego by telling you what effect you have on me!'

He gave her an immodest grin and turned his wheelchair slightly to introduce the figure standing respectfully behind.

'This is Haroun. He carries me to the water when I want to swim and tucks me up in bed at night.'

Vivienne had already noticed the incredible individual whom she had at first taken to be a servant. How could she miss him? He was bigger than Abdul with biceps almost as wide as her waist. He wore spotless cricket trousers, a cream string vest and a floppy turban and in a dusky oriental way he reminded her of a genial physical training instructor. Robert had described him lightly enough, but she gathered that Haroun watched over him night and day. The two of them had been engaged in a laughing conversation of sorts before her appearance and Robert explained, 'His English is about as good as my Arabic, but we get along. Right, Haroun?'

It was clear that the brown giant had no idea what was being said, but he responded readily enough in the booming tones of an amiable genie, 'That is so, Lord.'

'Take no notice of the title,' Robert said with his blue twinkle. 'He's an Ouarzate, and his tribe believe that all fair people are the true descendants of the Prophet. Trent had him brought from Marrakesh. I'm not exactly a lightweight and there was nobody locally willing to take on the job,' the handsome young invalid elucidated humorously and without a trace of self-pity. He shot something which sounded like, '*Là bàs aleyk*,' at the big Moor and as they both grinned he told Vivienne, 'Haroun's teaching me Arabic. I make noises like a camel clearing its throat, but I want to get the hang of it so I can learn something of his background.'

With so little time! Vivienne was careful to show no reaction, though Robert's courage had a way of humbling one. She was smiling along with him and making some lighthearted rejoinder when she saw Trent coming through an opening in the tall hibiscus hedge on the opposite side of the pool. He had obviously been walking close by and it struck her that he had probably engineered it so that he could witness her meeting with Robert, but at a distance. Her cheeks burned fleetingly, first with anxiety—had she played her part convincingly——? and then with indignation. Trust apparently did not come into Trent's scheme of things. Though she had to admit he looked disarming enough as he strolled round to join them.

In lemon-coloured slacks, superbly tailored of course, and a paisley-patterned silk shirt, he had that relaxed yet shrewd air of a man whose main strength is self-assurance. She guessed he was at least ten to fifteen years older than his brother. The difference showed in the heaviness of his build. His hair had only a light sprinkling of Robert's fairness so that in the sun it showed bronze streaks. There was no denying that he was attractive in a rough-hewn kind of way. But then, she reflected with an inward bitter smile, he had all the trappings on hand to give a man polish. How could he miss!

Of course she gave no sign that she had been taking all this in. Her dress crisp in the morning sunlight, the wide belt hugging her slender waist, she stood by striving to appear completely at ease as he aproached.

'Good morning, Vivienne.' His blue glance fenced with hers before moving on to the wheelchair where it straight away gleamed with lazy affection. 'Well, Rob, old son,' his tones were teasing, 'the gift pack safely delivered as I promised. How does it feel now you've untied the ribbon and taken a peep?'

'Great!' The younger brother reached out a hand to take hers. 'Viv's everything and more than I expected.' He looked up to explain to her with his grin, 'Trent wasn't keen to have a girl in the house. He's lived a bachelor existence for so long he's got choosy about who he allows into his domain.'

Vivienne told herself she much preferred the soft, youthful curve of his mouth to that hard excuse for a smile that was trained in her direction. 'I'll try not to get in his way,' she said with the same sort of ice that he applied, wrapped up of course in the ostensible warmth of friendship.

'Don't creep about on my account. I'm ready to concede that a woman about the place adds a decorative touch,' Trent replied suavely, drawing up a pool-side chair for her to sit in. He found one for himself, nodding pleasantly to Haroun and rattling off something, perhaps an Arabic 'good morning', before seating himself on the other side of his brother.

Robert wanted to hear all about Vivienne's arrival, how Trent had picked her up at the airport and brought her back to the house. They gave him the details between them, leaving out the tight-lipped lecture and the cool rejoinders in the car, and the unfriendly sparring at the dinner table. Even so Robert looked from one to the other while they talked as though he sensed something of the discord behind their smiles.

At the corner of the pool nearest the house there was a raised circular platform, a viewpoint no doubt, furnished for outdoor dining, and while they chatted together breakfast was being trolleyed out and arranged by the stately Abdul and the attendant who had waited on them at the dinner table. Instead of his dashing waistcoat of last night Momeen wore a starched white jacket over his silken pantaloons so that viewing the top half of him he looked rather like a dapper *maitre d'hôtel*, while the bottom half defied description. Vivienne could only assume that he was making a stern attempt with himself to become Westernised while at the same time still clinging in some ways to his comfortable Eastern garb. Abdul, of course, was wholly and unquestionably Arab.

A tray of glinting silverware signalled the arrival of the tea, and rising, Trent guided Vivienne before him while

Robert, who had been helped into a cotton bathrobe, was pushed in the wheelchair by his muscular aide. A ramp had been designed alongside the steps of the dining terrace and once the young invalid had been positioned at the table Haroun left them, presumably to have his own breakfast indoors.

Vivienne saw at once that the view was, as she had expected and dreaded, as strikingly lovely as it had been from her balcony. The sight of well-remembered haunts drove a shard of pain through her heart and foolishly, as she almost instantly realised, she chose a chair with her back to the low-walled parapet.

Trent, seeing her settled, commented with an ironic smile on his lips, 'As a female guest you're supposed to swoon at the amenities we have to offer here at Koudia, namely in this case, the first-hand view of the Casbah and the steamers in the harbour below.'

'I don't care for heights,' Vivienne replied smoothly, flicking open her table napkin. But far from being able to meet his gaze as he seated himself across from her it occurred to her in the next moment how dangerously near she had come to forgetting her role.

'You're joking, Viv.' Robert looked at her teasingly as he poured milk into his tea. 'We're no higher than an anthill up here. And what about that time you were winched up on a bale of hay at your dad's farm? You wrote me about it, remember?'

Trent's blue gaze on her was satirically enquiring. 'So you're a farmer's daughter?' He reached for a finger of toast, openly eyeing her slim shoulders and slender wrists.

'Not only that, she's got grit too,' Robert said proudly. 'Do you know what she did? Because no one else was available she rode up on a bundle of hay to the top of the gantry tower to free the pulley in the roof, full fifty feet from the ground. She didn't brag about it, but I guessed how it was from the way she wrote.'

'Plucky!' Trent agreed, raking her with his blue gleam.

'I don't work much around the farm now,' Vivienne said

quickly, fighting the colour that she knew was creeping up her throat into her cheeks. 'I haven't done for ages.'

She was glad that the trolley arrived at that moment to divert the attention away from her as the sizzling breakfast dishes were transferred to the table. And fortunately after that the conversation was merely the light chat that usually accompanies a meal.

It was a richly laid out table there on the little terrace where Japanese lilac and tiny button roses glowed against the blue sky. Besides grilled swordfish and other succulent seafood titbits, plus tender young lamb and chicken livers, there was honey from Valencia, the long black dates from south Morocco, green figs and tangerines. Vivienne guessed that the tantalising display was aimed at tempting Robert's indifferent appetite. He was keenly interested in the history of Tangier and without giving much thought to what he was eating he told her about a Britisher of the past, owner of a villa across the bay, who had kept open house for the country people on their way in and out of Tangier because the country Caids saved his life when he was captured by the brigand chieftain Raisuli.

He talked about anything and everything, boyishly eager to make her feel at ease and part of the household, and she very soon slipped into a more relaxed frame of mind. Momeen was on hand to serve when required. He was particularly attentive towards Vivienne, showing by his elaborate gestures and pearly smile that he too hoped she would stay for a while. Delicious though they were, she had to make a firm stand when it came to a second helping of the Tafilalet dates.

'Allow me, mademoiselle, to refill your dish with more of these droplets of sunshine.'

'They're a wonderful start to the day, Momeen, but I'm afraid I couldn't eat any more.'

'But Mademoiselle has swallowed less than a bird would need for its flight across the garden.'

'What bird is that, Momeen, a fat turkey perhaps? Or a waddling duck?'

She argued laughingly with him in his own tongue without giving it a thought. It was only afterwards that she realised what she had done.

Trent was watching her. He said lazily, 'You speak very good French, Vivienne.'

'Thank you,' she replied politely. But this time she made a determined effort to keep the colour from staining her cheeks. What was wrong with being able to converse in the language widely used in Tangier? Lots of people spoke French fluently. It was pure nerves, she told herself, making her imagine pitfalls where there weren't any.

After breakfast she thought Trent would disappear indoors, but much to her dismay he accompanied them back to the poolside, Haroun having returned by this time to take charge of the wheelchair, and from a briefcase which the manservant Abdul brought from the house, as though this was routine, he sat at the drinks table casually checking through business figures.

Vivienne took the chair next to Robert. She would have given anything for a brief respite. She could understand Trent wanting to spend every available moment with his brother, but it was singularly wearing on her to have to remain constantly on her guard. She needn't have worried. It hadn't dawned on her, but Robert too was finding the poolside a little overcrowded. Holding hands, they had only been sitting for a short time when he said with a restless grin, 'I think Viv and I will take a stroll, Trent. Maybe I could show her the grounds.'

Glancing up from his work, Trent said drily, with a mocking lift of an eyebrow, 'Don't mind me.'

Haroun came to take over the wheelchair, but with a pleading look at his brother Robert put in quickly, 'Viv can manage. I can turn the wheels a bit myself.'

Trent looked doubtful, but he said something and the Moor stepped back into the shadows. 'You and the chair make a considerable weight to push around, Rob,' he pointed out. 'The job might be too tough for Vivienne.'

'I'm sure I can manage,' Vivienne replied, taking charge

of the chair. She would gladly have had a go at pushing an
armoured tank to get away from Trent for a while!

Robert showed her the way and they went round the
pool and through the opening in the tall hibiscus hedge.
Beyond it was even more lovely than the section of the
grounds she had already seen. A fountain standing in a
star-shaped pool of cream tiles which in turn was set in a
richly coloured mosaic star, played musically in a spacious
area bordered by banana trees and palms. From here the
path led them into the deep shade where potted plants were
clustered beneath flowering vines, lianas and jasmine, then
out into the open past various lawned platforms and sweet-
scented flower-beds, some 'screened by the green lacework
of towering pepper trees, others by cedars, no less magnificent than their counterparts lining the drive.

They passed a domed summerhouse brilliantly white and
of Moorish design and mosaic benches tucked away in
arbours of oleander blossom and fragrant pelargonium, and
through the trees one caught glimpses of the fruit orchards,
a calm backwater above the city noises rising from among
the towers and bastions of the medina.

In the orange groves Vivienne could see Berber women
working among the trees. The smile playing about her lips
had a tartness about it. Trent must be very satisfied with
the niche he had carved for himself here in Tangier—with
other people's money. Living on the proceeds of the casino
didn't appear to trouble him at all.

There were banks of azaleas and asters and snow-white
viburnum where the gardens sloped away to the orchards,
but Robert wasn't interested in the view. He braked the
wheel of the chair at a spot where a patch of blue sea was
visible through the trees and turned. Vivienne felt her heart
start to accelerate. Now they were alone, and he would
want to pour out his heart to her. She could see it in his
eyes.

'Viv!' He grabbed her hand. 'At last we're together. Do
you know how long I've hungered for this moment?'

For the first time she caught a glimpse of fear and uncertainty in his blue gaze, a plea for help that touched at the very centre of her being so that she replied warmly, 'Robert, I want nothing but your happiness.'

'Kiss me, Viv. I need your love. Oh, how I need you here beside me!' He pulled her down to him and claimed her lips with passionate intensity. Vivienne recoiled, but only inwardly. The feel of a man's lips after all this time was like the flick of a whip on her emotions. Vivid pictures of Gary flew into her mind. Gary making some light remark and drawing her close to him. Gary brushing his lips lingeringly against hers. The torment of knowing that this wasn't Gary but someone else was almost too much to bear, and then at last Robert released her. Giving her a quizzical look as slowly she drew away from him, he said, his grin resuming its boyish slant, 'Not as forthcoming as your letters, but it will do for now.'

To hide the strain in her smile she ran her fingers through his blond thatch and asked, 'Who cuts your hair? You look like a well-fed island castaway.'

'Haroun chops it when it gets in my eyes in the water.' He thrust a hand through it. 'But you can cut it now. I promise to sit still like a good boy.' There was mischief in his eyes and yet gazing down into them she saw something else too, something much deeper. And as she stood drowning in the boyish sincerity there, with a catch at her heart she was sure of one thing. He mustn't be hurt. No matter what, Robert mustn't be hurt.

'I like it as it is,' she said, smoothing a hand over the corn-coloured locks, 'I don't want to change anything about you.' Groping for words as she was, she realised she might have said the wrong thing, although Robert gave no sign of having noticed. He took both her hands in his in that fervent yet gentle way of his, bottled-up emotion in his tones. 'Viv, my sweet, we're going to have a great time together. I'm not much good like this,' he looked down at the wheelchair, 'but wait till you see me in the pool. The water takes my weight and I can move as fast as anyone—so you'd better watch out!'

Aware of the glint in his eye, she responded playfully, 'I move pretty well myself. Maybe you won't catch me.'

'Oh yeah! I've an idea that's just bravado. I seem to recall you telling me in one of your letters that you didn't handle yourself too well in the water, apart from paddling around in the shallow end.'

Vivienne met his teasing look, hiding the minor jolt inside her with an appropriate smile. Why couldn't she remember what she had read in Lucy's letters? She would never win any medals for memorising facts, that was for sure! 'I've been doing quite a bit of practising,' she said airily. 'Now I'm quite a competent swimmer.'

'Is that a fact?' He eyed her with bemused wonder. He still held her hands in his and drawing her gently down to sit on the arm of his chair he changed the subject, with a satisfied grin. 'When did you first know you were in love with me?'

Vivienne hoped he couldn't feel the blood thumping through her. When? When? She searched distractedly in her mind and replied lightly, 'Oh, very early on. Almost from the start.'

A look of disappointment passed fleetingly over his face. 'You can't have forgotten that week!' His grin was lopsided. 'I sent you a sprig of orange blossom, remember? And you pressed it beside some winter lavender and sent it to me in a booklet of poems ... *To hear the lark begin his flight and singing, startle the dull night,*' he quoted softly.

Vivienne had never heard the words. She laughed flounderingly. 'Well, of course! But I'm here now and I'm more concerned with the present.'

Luckily she had saved the situation by saying what came naturally. Robert put an arm around her waist and squeezed her against him. The smile he gave her was still somewhat lopsided as he remarked, 'For a girl who's so good to look at you've got a lousy memory. But I won't hold it against you. I love you anyway.'

She brushed her lips against his temple, partly with relief and partly, strangely enough, with a choking feeling of affection. But the subject was altogether too dangerous to pursue and as casually as she could she manoeuvred the conversation on to other things. 'Do the women always water the trees like that?' She pointed to where the plump, swathed figures were building up little bastions of mud.

'They do it to deflect the flow from one channel to another,' Robert nodded. 'That way every tree gets its share.' He went on to tell her about work on the estate generally, how the plum orchard would soon be a riot of blossom, and about the marketing of a special, heavily-scented narcissus. And Vivienne listened eagerly. While the talk remained general she had no worries. It was only when Robert, still finding it hard to contain his excitement at having her with him, occasionally swung the conversation back to them. But during these precarious moments she managed to carry things along by chattering about what they were going to do in the days ahead, and so avoiding further blunders.

The sun was high overhead when they made their way back to the house. Robert showed her a different route which took them through a mildly mysterious and altogether enchanting area where high crumbling walls, festooned with blossom, surrounded a ruined pavilion. Tall and slender and of pink sun-baked brick, it was curiously Mongol in appearance with what must have been big glazed windows and other features clearly defined. The third floor had the air of a summer house and probably commanded quite a view of the city.

'Trent says it's a *minzah*, built in the old days for the entertainment of guests,' Robert smiled at her enthralled look and indicated the agitated fluttering from within. 'Right now the only guests are the local pigeons.'

They left the birds in peace and went through a festooned opening. Here the dark waters of a square pool reflected the surrounding overgrown greenery, stone urns sprouting weeds and on the far side the slender pillared archways of another crumbling interior. The silence was overwhelming. In the antique simplicity of the place

Vivienne could imagine a dancer of the past clad in colourful veils, flitting alongside the pool on her way to entertain
the guests in the *minzah*.

They took a path through a mimosa thicket and were
soon back at the house. Vivienne handed Robert over to
Haroun and went upstairs to her room limp, not with ex-
haustion, for she had experienced no difficulty in guiding
the wheelchair along the level paths, but with the strain of
saying and doing all the right things. There was little time
for shedding the tension, however, for no sooner had she
freshened up and run a comb through her hair than the
lunch gong, a muffled oriental clang, sounded through the
house.

Where they were to eat she had no idea; she only prayed
that Trent had business to attend to, or that he would be
lunching in some other part of the house.

Robert was waiting for her downstairs with Haroun, who
flashed her his amiable grin, in attendance. They went
along the hall which ran parallel with the front of the house
to the adjoining tower in the Moorish mansion, passing
painted chests and Berber sculpture and catching glimpses
through open doorways of the shady archways lining the
front terrace. It was in the left wing, in a richly furnished
circular room with an outlook on to a small private garden
fragrant with roses and gardenias, that the meal was to be
taken. And Vivienne's heart sank when she moved into the
room. Trent, his usual urbane self, greeted them pleasantly, 'Had a good morning?' and guided her to a chair at
the table.

She noted the elegant display of china and crystal-ware,
the central sweet-smelling posy, and guessed that all this
was done for Robert's sake; the constant changes of scene
to ward off the staleness of being confined to the house, the
gay touches to keep his spirits up. In other words no expense was spared to provide him with pleasing distractions.
She felt a flicker of irritation course through her. Why
couldn't Trent run true to form? He didn't mind taking
money from gullible gamesters, yet beneath that suave

veneer he watched over his ailing brother with a tenderness and affection that was, darn it, almost touching.

The food, naturally, the best in French cuisine, suffered no loss of flavour on its journey from the kitchen in the other wing. Vivienne knew vaguely that every forkful melted in the mouth, but she was too on edge wondering what would crop up in the conversation to come anywhere near to enjoying it.

Their morning together had put Robert in a buoyant mood. Fortunately he appeared quite content to spar playfully with his brother. 'How was business last night, Trent? Spot any duchesses in disguise at the Café Anglais?'

'Not a one. Unless I slipped up on the guy in the turbanned headgear of a camel driver,' Trent said with a grin like his brother's, Vivienne thought, only more worldly.

Robert told her, 'Trent's casino is typically Moroccan—caged parrots on the wall, fringed lampshades over the tables. I saw it when we first arrived. And the clientele's a mixture of fez-wearing Arabs and European jean-clad royalty.' He toyed with the buttered aubergines on his plate and added impishly, 'You can get anything from a cup of tea to a stiff French brandy at the Café Anglais and have a flutter in the adjoining gaming rooms with chips ranging from ten pence to a thousand pounds in the local currency.'

'All on a one-way journey into the family coffers, of course,' Vivienne put in lightly, flashing a spirited look Trent's way.

'Meaning that fools and their money are soon parted.' Just as lightly his smile matched hers for veiled antagonism. He shrugged. 'Everyone has a fair chance. The bank can win, but it can lose too.'

'And it's not shackled with principles,' Vivienne tacked on smoothly. 'It doesn't concern itself with, say, ruined homes and bankrupt businesses.' Despite her efforts to appear in joking mood for Robert's sake, she felt her insides trembling at this clash with Trent.

He helped himself to more claret before replying lazily, 'Gambling is coeval with human nature. I twist no one's arm. In running a casino all I do is provide a means for the sport.'

'I think I would call it a subtle pandering to the weaknesses of humanity.' Her breath was coming fast. She wished she didn't feel so strongly about what didn't concern her anyway.

'You're eloquent in your argument, Vivienne,' Trent commented suavely. 'Unfortunately you're a woman and the fairer sex invariably see a gaming club as a House of Sin ... a magician's trap for catching souls,' she felt that he was teasing her in a steely way, 'whereas to a man it has something which appeals to all the senses.'

'Except, perhaps, common sense.' To disguise the jarring note between her and Trent, though she had a feeling that Robert wasn't fooled, she added laughingly, 'And I insist on having the last word. Anyway, to my mind Tangier is too nice a place to be spoiled with that kind of entertainment.'

The sting in the tail of her comment was quashed urbanely by Trent's smiling reply, 'Every Eden has its serpent,' and his implication, of course, that *he* meant to have the last word.

Robert intervened at that moment to bring the time to their notice. 'Hey, it's almost two! Tell Momeen to chop-chop with the sweet, Trent. I want to show Viv how I can move in the pool.' With his mind on the outdoors the conversation was spasmodic after that, and less harrowing, for Vivienne at least.

Haroun returned from his own meal and Trent insisted that Robert be wheeled away for his usual after-lunch rest before venturing near the pool. Vivienne managed to snatch a little time to herself in her room, but the hour flew by and soon she was hunting through her things as Robert yodelled up from below that he was on his way.

Lucy had flung everything she could find in the suitcase, and that included a satin bikini and a lime-coloured figure-moulding swimsuit. In the latter under a towelling robe Vivienne made her way to the pool. Robert was already in the water and she suspected he hadn't wanted her to see

Haroun carrying him from the wheelchair. Now the big
Moor padded around the pool's circumference with orders,
no doubt, to be ready at a moment's notice should his
young charge require assistance.

Vivienne felt shy of disrobing, especially as Trent was
sitting at his table near the sun umbrellas quietly flicking
through business papers. But Robert, treading water and
showing off, was noisily insistent and she had no choice but
to drop her things on a chair and go and join him. With
her hair wet and plastered in curls about her face, there was
no room for worry after that. A pair of muscular arms
scooped her up and tossed her playfully over the glistening
surface, and laughter spurted from her as she set about giving Robert a run for his money.

His brute strength astounded her. Though she swam
with all the force she could muster, fairly zipping up the
length of the pool, he was ahead of her, bobbing up in no
time and extracting strangled laughter from her as she
wrested from his powerful grasp to beat him to the side.
That was only the start of his antics. He was determined, it
seemed, to show her every trick he knew in the water,
which inevitably involved a ducking for him or for her.

Being chased, tossed up and down, and losing every race,
she was exhausted but curiously light. It came to her that
there was no fear of saying the wrong thing splashing about
hilariously in the water; no dread of making a disastrous
reply to one of Robert's remarks, or tripping up where
Trent was concerned. It was pleasant to trundle on one's
back and gaze up at the blue sky and for the first time since
arriving at Koudia some of the agonising strain left her.

But like all good things the afternoon came to an end.
Vivienne and Robert lounged in inflated armchairs in the
pool and drank long drinks, but it was obvious that he was
tiring and as the sun started to lower Trent rose and holding her wrap called, 'Come and dry off, Vivienne. It will be
cool in another half hour.'

His tones brooked no argument and meekly she left her

chair and swam obediently to the side. He reached a hand
down to tug her up and with her fingers in his firm grasp
she felt the vitality in him course through her. He threw the
robe round her shoulders, holding it there as though to dry
her. Her gaze locked momentarily with his. When she
turned Haroun had his charge in the wheelchair and in his
soft-footed, hefty manner was leisurely making his way
round to them.

Robert was happy, but a little grey-faced and clearly
quite resigned to retiring to his room. 'See you tomorrow,
Viv. It's been a wonderful day. I can't wait for sun-up!' He
pulled her down to him and kissed her on the lips, after
which she felt obliged to follow him and Haroun to the
house. She was hopeful that she too could withdraw to the
blissful sanctuary of her room for the night until Trent's
formal tones came from behind, 'Dinner will be at the
usual time, Vivienne. I'll see you then.'

Up in her room she knew, with a grim little smile, that
he intended to keep her under the microscope of his attention until he was satisfied with her motives. She washed
the pool water out of her hair and while it dried she tried
to take an interest in the magazine she had bought on the
journey out, without much success. When the time came to
go down to dinner she was still battling to overcome her
trepidation at having to dine alone with Trent. Drat the
man! Why did she allow him to unnerve her like this? It
was true she was playing a game of deceit, but not for the
reasons he suspected.

She found him waiting for her in the room overlooking
the dimly-lit rooftops of the Casbah, where they had dined
last night. He was dressed for the Casino in faultless evening wear. Her white skirt and sleeveless coffee-coloured
blouse seemed a little out of place beside so much polish,
though she didn't let that worry her as he came to draw out
a chair for her at the table.

She knew that she had not been apprehensive without
cause, for no sooner had they sat down to face each other
across the gleaming expanse than he was saying with his

razor-edged smile, 'Congratulations, Vivienne. You appear to have Robert in the palm of your hand.'

The resentment seethed in her. She was itching to make a retort that would deflate his judicial conceit, but keeping the image of Lucy firmly to the forefront of her mind she replied evenly, 'I'm glad you approve.' He filled her glass with wine, and she saw the glint of irony in his eyes at the smooth way she had sidestepped the issue.

Momeen, in Eastern jacket of lurid design, was as usual on top form, marching in and out with dishes that gave him a pride to serve. He had no qualms in front of Trent and prattled away in French about the excellence of the *soupe au pistou* and the perfection of the *croquettes Parisienne*.

Vivienne didn't make the mistake of showing too much knowledge of the language, although the damage had been done in that direction and there was nothing she could do to repair it. The worst of it was she got the impression that Trent's thoughts were running on the same lines as her own. In between the appearance of new dishes he baited her with his granite-like humour. 'You swim amazingly well, Vivienne—almost as though you once spent most of your time lazing beside the water.'

'I learnt most of what I know at school,' she said above the feathering of her breath in her throat.

'Of course. And that's where you became so proficient at French.'

'No.' She smiled across at him to fox him. 'I picked that up later.' And carried away with the exhilaration of crossing him, she added with a lift of her chin, 'I speak Spanish too.'

'You do surprise me. Both languages widely used in Tangier.'

The colour rushed into her face. How easily he could trip her up! Over the confusion inside her she commented offhandedly, 'Some people have a knack for picking up a foreign tongue. I happen to be one of them.'

'And you're only a farmer's daughter!' the suave tones marvelled.

'There are farmers and farmers,' she commented smoothly.

He took in the neat simplicity of her blouse and skirt, the gleaming, uncomplicated hair-style that needed no expensive trips to the hairdressers, and drawled, 'That's right, there are.'

All through the meal Vivienne juggled with this kind of conversation. She felt like a mouse between the paws of a very astute and courteously smiling cat. It was hanging on to Lucy's image that kept her own smile intact, although it wasn't altogether for her friend's sake that she made all the right replies. There was something about this man that brought out the fight in her and she was determined not to let Lucy down if only for that reason.

After the dessert and coffee she would have given anything to fly with relief from the room and shut herself in upstairs, but her common sense told her to linger, and leisurely, as though she had nothing to fear in Trent's presence, she wandered to take in the starlit panorama. The wide windows were open and above the distant roar of the traffic in the city there was the whispered heaving of the sea along the shore and close at hand the sound of night birds calling to one another across the garden. Vivienne inhaled the cool air, clutching at the peace out there and wishing she were part of it. Trent strolled to her side. She was aware that he was sliding one of those capable brown hands into the inside pocket of his jacket for the gold cigarette case he carried and offering her one he asked, 'What was your father's reaction to your coming out here?'

Her head lowered to the flame he held for her. Her mind spun. Lucy's father? She doubted whether he had any knowledge of his daughter's letter writing. Looking up, she said, idly exhaling smoke, 'I'm old enough to please myself in these matters.'

'True,' he conceded with his tight grin and a shrug of his impeccably clad shoulders. And focussing that shrewd blue glance on her, 'I'd say you were around Rob's age. Am I right?'

'Almost. I'm twenty-three.' That at least was true.

He studied her from his position beside the brocaded curtains and commented lazily, 'Bit late by modern standards, isn't it? I thought girls entered into the marriage market at a much earlier age these days.'

'We don't all rush out to find a man, the minute we've put our school books away,' she cooed with barely disguised distaste. And giving him the same raking appraisal that he had given her, she added, 'And what about you? You're way past the bargaining stage for any woman. Thirty-five, I'd say ... or thirty-six.'

'Thirty-seven,' he corrected easily. And pulling on his cigarette, 'My life has been pretty full up to now, for the most part taken up with business. For this reason I've always kept women at a distance.'

'Am I to take it there are no women gamblers?' Vivienne feigned surprise. 'Every Eden has its serpent,' she mocked, tapping her cigarette on the ash-tray he offered before tacking on, 'and its innumerable Eves, no doubt?' She didn't know why, but the picture of svelte-clad females milling around Trent at the Casino somehow rasped on her nerves.

'Enough to make life interesting,' he drawled with an irritating self-satisfied glint. She didn't like the trend the conversation was taking, but she was helpless to do anything about it as he eyed her with his next remark, 'And while we're on the subject, wouldn't it be an idea to show Rob a little more warmth when you kiss him goodnight?'

Vivienne was stunned by his words. She fought back the hot flush creeping up her throat and murmured a genuine excuse, 'This is our first day. I may have been writing to him for a long time, but I hardly know him as a person.'

'Funny, Rob doesn't seem to feel that way. He's young and emotionally bubbling over, and I get the idea that he'd like you to be the same.'

'I'll get round to it in time,' Vivienne had recovered enough to say lightly. 'I love Robert, but he's a little overpowering and all for sweeping me off my feet.'

'You'll handle him.' Trent looked from the end of his

cigarette to her. 'I'd say you know your way around, Vivienne.'

'You could be right,' she replied carelessly. 'But then perhaps not as much as you. *I've* no idea what the inside of a casino looks like.' And because she was almost at the end of her tether she pointed out smoothly, 'And by the way, isn't it time you were going to count up the chips?'

He looked at his watch. 'Thanks for reminding me,' he said drily. And as he turned to go, 'Don't feel you must spend the evenings shut in your room. You've got the run of the house, and there are plenty of good books in the library—the first door on your left out of here.'

'I'll wander in there if I may,' she murmured politely, going out with him. He said goodnight to her in the hall and a few minutes later she heard him leave in the big black limousine.

In the library, though its antique elegance was soothing to the eye, she couldn't shake off the tension which threatened to snap her in two. She thought that by losing herself in a book she would be able to unwind a little, but her mind was taut with strain and the words danced meaninglessly before her eyes. What a day it had been for her, cloaked as it were in Lucy's personality. Going over it in her mind she felt, with some small relief, that Robert accepted her as the writer of the letters, the girl who was in love with him. But what about Trent? Had she managed to fool him just as effectively? If only she knew!

CHAPTER THREE

THOUGH there were times when Vivienne wanted to flee from the lie she was living, some of the strain of those first days began to diminish as she fell in with the routine at Koudia. Each evening Abdul drove Trent into the city in the big black limousine and she was left to her own devices. Through the day, most of which she spent with Robert, she grew more accustomed to her surroundings and in lighter moments discovered a little about the various members of the household.

The magician in the kitchen, she learned, was a French chef called Maurice who lived in semi-retirement in a hotel suite in town, but spent most of his time at Koudia to oblige Trent. Every day Momeen went down to the Casbah to give his wife, who still clung to the yashmak and *haik*, money to buy food for herself and the children. Haroun, with his big grin, was a patient, if slow, teacher and it wasn't long before Vivienne had mastered the long and complicated greetings in Arabic.

Her biggest worry was when she was alone with Trent and Robert. There was always the danger of making a reply which didn't coincide with what the younger brother expected her to say, and Trent, she knew, missed nothing. Once a week Robert spent a day at the hospital undergoing blood tests and examinations. Vivienne passed the time on these occasions wandering on her own in the grounds. The tranquil beauty of the place with its palm tree corners and spreading cedars never failed to act as balm on her stretched nerves. At the rear of the Moorish villa she discovered the household garages. Gathering dust there was a low-slung expensive racing machine in a rich metallic wine colour. She supposed sadly that it had been Robert's once and that his brother made no use of it for this reason. Taking advantage of the time she had to herself, she locked herself in her room and wrote long letters to Lucy giving a detailed account of all that had happened so far. These she gave to Momeen to post when he was on his way to town.

The afternoons in the pool ought to have been the most relaxing time of day for her. Splashing about with Robert, laughing at his antics, she had only to be herself. Yet it was impossible to remain oblivious to Trent's presence, sitting as he did at the table near the sun umbrellas, occasionally lifting his glance from his papers to follow the fun.

She grew fond of Robert; how could she help it? Young and eager though he was, he had a gentleness that was touching. And his illness seemed to have given him a sensitivity and maturity far beyond his years. He never spoke of the awful fate that awaited him, except on one occasion when they touched on it accidentally in conversation. They were sitting in their favourite spot overlooking the fruit orchards one morning. Vivienne saw how the sun lit up the tall white buildings of Tangier and listening to the distant commotion in the streets she said spontaneously, 'It's a pity I can't take you for a walk down there for a change of scene. I'm sure I would handle the wheelchair very well.'

'Trent wouldn't allow it,' Robert shrugged easily. He added drily, 'According to the doctors I stand a better chance of hanging on to the time I've got left if I stick to the fresh air and peace around Koudia.'

Vivienne could have cut out her tongue, but the moment passed and soon they were talking about other things.

The one time she dreaded most was in the evening when she was obliged to dine alone with Trent. She often tried to pluck up the courage to say that she would prefer to take the meal in her room, but she knew that Trent used the occasions to sound her out as to how the day had gone and she dared not arouse his suspicions by appearing indifferent. As they talked of Robert his manner were merely that of an affectionate older brother. It was the little things, the deep lines etched around his mouth, the premature dusting of grey at his temples, that told her of his crushing frustration and grief.

Most of the time her fears that he would stumble on to the fact that she was an impostor were unfounded. He treated her courteously, often offering her a cigarette at the end of the meal and whiling away the time before he left for the casino by joining her at the window to contemplate the view. Only when she heard him drive away did she truly feel safe in discarding the Lucy pose.

As Vivienne Blyth she found the evenings were long. She spent the best part of them on the balcony outside her room. And as she stood there under the star-strewn sky staring down at the blurred buildings of the old town, it seemed to her that she was living two lives, one where she gave all her time and attention to Robert, the other where she dreamed here over the view, every part of her yearning for Gary.

At first just being here in Tangier with all its heart-shattering memories had been almost too much for her. Now she found herself brooding nightly over the familiar sights, striving to recapture in her mind some of the golden moments of that summer four years ago. Soon it wasn't enough just to look at the twinkling lights of the wide avenues, to listen to the muffled cacophony of sound rising from the Medina. She wanted to become a part of the life in the city sprawling at the foot of the sloping orchards of Koudia, to feel Gary in the noisy narrow alleys of the Casbah, in the scent of charcoal burning stoves, jasmine wands sold on rickety stalls, donkeys with laden panniers and the café tables in the crowded Socco Chico.

Well, why not? It came to her one evening that she was perfectly free to do as she pleased. Robert was in his own quarters with Haroun keeping a watch in case he needed anything. The rest of the house was in semi-darkness with no one to care what she did; Momeen least of all, who stayed glued to the television set in the servants' section.

Her mind made up, she went in from the balcony and put on a pair of suitable shoes. The air was warm, but just in case it dropped chilly she picked up a light cardigan with her handbag. Downstairs the lights in the impressive hall with its Moorish and French decor shone to themselves. Vivienne was soon leaving them behind as she stepped quickly along the drive. She had only to follow the road through the fruit orchards. She reckoned she could be in town in about half an hour.

It was not much after that when her footsteps were taking her along the Rue de la Casbah. But time meant nothing to her now. She was lost in the bustle of traffic and people, soaking up the well-remembered feel of the place, her blood tingling at familiar rendezvous and landmarks. Like an avid tourist she made for the street of the Great Mosque, ignoring the patter from the would-be guides, shuffling figures in dirty caftans and knitted skullcaps, pretending to know the sights. *'Par ici, mademoiselle,' 'Je vous conduirai partout.'*

She had learned a long time ago how to deal with them and with a firm word she put them behind her. Along the narrow Rue des Siaghines, the Street of the Jewellers, business was being transacted in that feverish way peculiar to the East. The Indian shops glittered with exotic goods from overseas. There were watches everywhere, from wrist to elbow on the grinning pedlars, the more expensive ones winking behind plate glass in brightly lit interiors overshadowing the money-changers' doorways and stalls adorned with cheap necklaces.

To Vivienne the crowded thoroughfare was like a drug on her senses. She pushed ahead with her eyes on the faces of the passers-by, her heart knocking in the old familiar way. Suppose she was to see him! Suppose they were to meet again after all this time! She looked dreamily through an old crone who thrust a tray of gaudy bracelets at her. Gary always said he would never leave Tangier. It was she who had left. She had flown back to England to try and forget him. Now as she walked the streets of the town, *their* town, it seemed like only yesterday.

She came to the Socco Chico, the plaza lined with café

tables. It was as she had always remembered it, choked with people of all nationalities, the tables crowded and the air reverberating with the babble of Spanish, Arabic and French. She found a seat with the ornate grillework of a window behind her and ordered a Cinzano. The drink, when it arrived, tasted strange to her lips after so long, but its acid fragrance was so evocative of the past it brought a sharp sparkle of tears to her eyes. She and Gary had drunk Cinzano all the time. And now as she watched the flow of passers-by, a mixture of *djellaba*-clad and Western-attired strollers, it was almost as though she had never been away.

She had been on holiday that summer when she had first met Gary. She was a member of a package tour party and he played the saxophone in the hotel dance band. During one of his breaks from the stage he had asked her to dance with him and from then on things had snowballed between them. She had liked his dark, good-looking features, the way his hair grew back from his rather high forehead, giving him a learned, studious air. She soon learned that looks could be deceiving. Gary was gay and adventurous by nature. He told her he had taught himself to play the saxophone, which was why, she suspected, his renderings when he stood up to play his solos on the stage lacked any real depth or feeling. He was really only interested in paying his way in Tangier.

When her two weeks' holiday was up she was too wildly in love with Gary to think of leaving. Recklessly she went and got a job in one of the tourist agencies on the Rue du Statut, and a cheap room to rent, and the package tour party went back without her. She never regretted her decision to stay on. Gary was the perfect companion. They spent the summer lounging on the beach and, when they had time off together, visiting all the exotic places she had only read about: Marrakesh, set so dramatically against the snow-capped Atlas mountains, Rabat, with its ancient medinas, and the fabulous market places of Fez. In the evenings Gary had shown her the night life of Morocco.

They had been true Arabian nights for Vivienne.

Then things had started to go wrong. Gary lost his job with the hotel dance band. He became moody. He had always wanted her to live with him in the tiny apartment he rented, but some small part of her held out against that. She always had a feeling that her refusal to go the whole way in their lovemaking had something to do with the break-up. Gary had never been one to bother much about finesse. He told her one day in the street that he didn't see much point in their going on together and after a brief farewell, though she begged him to think it over, he turned and walked away.

As she watched him become lost in the crowd, knowing there was no point in calling him back, Vivienne had swayed at the blow. Her whole world had become Gary. She never woke in the morning without thinking first of him, never closed her eyes at night without seeing his rakish grin. How could she face life without him?

Numbed as she was, it was some days before she could bring herself to think clearly. Then she had packed her things and taken a plane to England and oblivion. But it hadn't been easy to forget. She closed her eyes now in the crowded plaza, knowing that if Gary were to appear in front of her at this moment the four years would dissolve and she would fall into his arms.

She was taken for a tourist at the tables, and though there were many visitors out seeing the sights a girl on her own was not altogether usual and naturally she was pestered. 'Would Mademoiselle care to see a most unusual performance in the Place de la Plage? I am free. For a small fee I would consider it a pleasure to guide you there.' Robed men of dubious countenance gave her their gold-toothed smiles. She decided it was time to move on. She took the route along the narrow alleyways adjoining the Rue des Siaghines, between tiny shops packed with the doubtful treasures of Africa, and then because it was growing late she turned back towards Koudia.

The house was unchanged when she re-entered. The

lights still shone on the camel-hair chests, the wall daggers and hanging brocades in the long hall. Quickly she went up to her room and drawing the curtains across the tall windows overlooking the balcony she undressed for bed.

Now the days were not so trying. It was true there was always a certain amount of strain walking in Lucy's shoes where Robert was concerned, and having to sit and chat under Trent's speculative gaze, but now she had the evenings to look forward to, and there was always a chance—oh, breathless moment—that she would run into Gary. It was no use fooling herself; she knew that now. Those long, lonely four years had done nothing to erase the memory of Gary from her mind. She used the nights to comb the city, hoping ... hoping ...

Nobody noticed her going or her return. Dining with Trent in the evenings she forced herself to stifle the eager anticipation inside her, sharing a leisurely cigarette with him after the meal and striving to appear utterly cool and composed. She would allow half an hour after he had left and then start out on her own in search of Gary.

Though their favourite haunts had been the old town, she began after a while to explore the brightly lit avenues of modern Tangier, drifting past the tourist offices with their gay postered windows inducing one to travel ... travel, alongside art and camera shops, elegant restaurants and stores. Once or twice she wandered along the Boulevard Pasteur, staring into the Hotel Riadh as she went by. It was shabbier than she remembered it but still popular with visitors, for the foyer always seemed to be busy. She recognised one of the male receptionists behind the desk from her stay there four years ago, but he probably wouldn't remember her.

Walking along the modern routes was much more tiring, and sometimes she would sit on one of the benches in the Promenade Gardens. There was no real chance, however, to scan the faces of the passers-by coming from the Avenida de España, for she was invariably pestered by some shady individual spinning her an implausible tale. Also she felt closer to Gary in the narrow alleyways of the old town and the Casbah.

She had never, as yet, been to the Casbah on her own, but one evening it occurred to her that that might be the very place where she ought to go. Within those fortress walls, with its ancient Moorish palaces, winding passage-ways choked with biblical characters, truly of the East, Gary had loved to roam. She could see him now, as she hurriedly slipped out of the dress she had worn for dinner, with the stubble of a beard on his chin, fingering his drink at one of the old café tables in his favourite haunt. He had always said laughingly that he would die in the Casbah.

A little feverishly she donned a linen skirt and a rose-pink blouse. Its shirt collar she left open at the throat, but the long sleeves fastened snugly at the wrists and this would prove a blessing later when the night air turned chilly. Her hands trembled a little as she touched up her make-up. She wanted to go out looking her best tonight. There was a flut-tering inside her. She wondered happily if she was slightly clairvoyant and therefore sensed that something stupendous was going to happen tonight.

She made her way downstairs with extra special care. Her cautiousness, however, was quite unnecessary. The elegant Moorish villa had that unlived-in atmosphere which it wore in the evenings when Trent was out and Robert shut away in his own rooms. Vivienne could smell the de-parture of the limousine on the drive when she went out. Remnants of the exhaust fumes still lingered on the air, a faint acrid thread mingling with the light perfume of fruit blossoms. But the car had had a good half-hour's start and it would take her more than that again to get down into town on foot, so she was safe until midnight or later. She had no idea what time Trent returned from the casino, but she guessed it was in the early hours of the morning.

It took her longer than she expected to reach the Casbah. The route, through a maze of back streets, was hazy in her mind and she made several wrong turnings before arriving at the Marshan Gate. Once inside the old walls she could

afford to dawdle. Though business was over for the day
donkeys laden with huge bales of fresh mint for the morning market straddled the alleyways, and from the tiny shop
doorways came wafts of cinnamon and cloves, paprika and
thyme. Children, thin-limbed with eyes like glowing black
buttons, darted about under her feet, and snatched playfully at her clothing, though they ought to have been in bed
hours ago. She peeped into tiny barn-like rooms where she
knew that during the day a dozen or more of these children would crowd cross-legged on the floor learning the
Koran from some old sage. Women in black robes and
yashmaks slid along the passageways and turban-wearing
men with grizzly beards and gappy smiles sat on the steps
of old Moorish inns solving the world's problems, as men
will.

Here inside the true walled enclosure of the native
quarter it was rather like being part of one big happy family,
but as it grew late and the alleys became deserted Vivienne
began to wonder if she had been wise in coming to the
Casbah at night time. Several well-to-do properties
bordered the area and she knew that the owners were compelled to employ watchmen, for thievery and skulduggery
was rife in this network of narrow lanes. And yet, even
though it was much later than she had planned to stay out,
something drove her on. She couldn't leave now, not without first browsing a little round the Casbah square, where
most of the Moorish cafés were situated. She hadn't seen
a Western face all evening, but the square was the meeting
place of all kinds of individuals, intellectuals, foreign re-
sidents in Tangier, and here more than anywhere there
was the possibility of ... She quickened her steps, too
tense with excitement to allow herself to think clearly. She
only knew that the square was where she must go.

Her footsteps echoed over the cobbles as she passed old
palaces and crumbling historic buildings. In some places
the upper storeys of the tall leaning houses jutted out overhead, shutting out all views of the velvet dark sky. It was
on the corner of one of these lanes that she spotted what

she had been looking for all evening: the sign which read *Rue de Riad*. This, she clearly recollected, was the way she and Gary used to go to the Casbah square. Her pulses suddenly began to quicken, not with fear because she had been thinking of Gary, and foolishly her heart had leapt into her throat as a figure had appeared at her side. But it was only a young Moor about sixteen years old and clearly he wanted nothing but to do a little business. He thrust a small skin drum, typical of the district, at her, and spoke in French, 'The pretty mademoiselle is looking for a gift?'

'Not now. It's much too late.' She answered him in English and pushed on. She knew that tourists were advised to hire an official Moorish guide when sightseeing in the Casbah, because the boys could be a nuisance. But now, at this time of night. Did they never sleep!

This one, a felt skullcap on his black curls, his white teeth gleaming in the shadows, was persistent.

'You American,' he said in broken English. 'You buy. Very cheap.'

'I'm not American. I'm English and I'm in a hurry.' She hoped that he would take the hint that she was not loaded with dollars.

'Okay, so I tell to you the money in English,' he quipped with a shrug of his shoulders. 'You give me five pounds now, okay?'

Vivienne walked on.

'Three pounds. I take now. It enjoys me very much to make this gift.'

Sidestepping the skipping figure, she could hear the sounds of the square not far away.

'Fifteen dirhams ...' The youth was growing anxious. 'Ten dirhams ...'

She would have liked to stop and tell him that she had no use for the drum, but she knew better than to become involved or this would be taken for bargaining, and they had now reached the square.

Her first reaction as she moved out into the lamplit space where creepers and trees showed their blossom above courtyard walls was one of acute disappointment. There were not many customers seated at the café tables and most of these seemed to be the type who had nowhere to sleep. There was a kind of sluggish activity over near some fruit crates where preparations were being made for the morning market, and one or two boys wheeled about dangerously on decrepit bikes, but this was not the square as she remembered it on her outings with Gary. She could see that the café society, the colourful types of her own kind, had left long ago.

She looked at her watch and was horrified to discover that it was almost one o'clock. She would have to return to Koudia without delay. *Without delay in this maze of streets?* Impulsively she turned to the felt-capped youth who was still by her side and asked, 'Do you know a quick way out of here? I must return to my friends.' She had pretended she was not alone for her own protection. Even so she sensed that the youth was swift to detect the uncertainty in her, though he replied smilingly enough, 'The Casbah is my home. Its pathways are as the veins of my hand.' He threw the drum to one of the bike youths and said something in rapid Arabic before beckoning her to follow him.

They crossed the square. Vivienne was conscious of the curious glances directed her way and knew that her light skirt and blouse were glaringly out of place among the djellabah-clad onlookers. She was almost relieved to be back in the dim alleys again until she noticed that there were one or two other mysterious figures flitting along in the shadows behind her. Weaving through the network of passageways, she soon realised that the bike youths were following their friend, and cheekily they came alongside her. 'Dollarés, dollarés ... American!' they chanted impishly.

She clutched her handbag tightly against her—another mistake, she realised as soon as she had done it. Why give the appearance of carrying a lot of money when all she possessed was a few dirhams? Her young guide grinned as the youths jostled her with exaggerated clumsiness, and she wondered what he expected to get out of it. Thankfully she saw the gate out into the Medina up ahead and breathed a sigh of relief.

There was a little more life outside the archway. Cars trundled over the cobbled surfaces and some of the *fondouks*—the local inns—were still open. Not far away Vivienne could see the lit frontages of hotels and places of entertainment down near the sea, and as she moved towards them she had high hopes of shaking off her playful begging acquaintances. She planned to give their leader, the one who had guided her out of the Casbah, a small reward for his trouble, but it was he who, first having satisfied himself that she had indeed no friends waiting for her, took the initiative. They were passing an old domed monument of some sect or other when, with the skill and deftness of a monkey, he whipped her handbag from under her arm and tossed it to a friend. With a grin, this one, well out of her reach, proceeded to open it and rummaged with a theatrical frown inside. Vivienne was not unduly frightened, only angry. They could take the money if they were so intent on having it, but there were other things inside her handbag, more precious than money, reminders of Gary, little odd-ments she had kept.

'Give that back to me at once!' she snapped, her cheeks blazing. By this time the cash had been discovered and with sneers distorting their grins at the paltry amount now in their possession the Moorish youths were not in too good a mood. Besides, the handbag was evidence and must dis-appear with the money. The leader got it back and waved it tantalisingly under her nose. That would teach her to fool them into believing that she was a rich tourist.

'Give it to me, do you hear!' She snatched crossly and got only a curled smile for a reply, and snatched again only to come up against another grinning member of the gang.

She was on the point of tears when a voice edged with steel uttering vitriolic Arabic cut sharply across the space. She was riveted by the sound. She had heard those tones somewhere before . . . at the airport terminal!

The youths' heads pivoted all in one direction, then with the stealth of night creatures they scattered and disappeared. There were people in the vicinity who carefully turned a blind eye to the incident, but it was the sight of a groomed figure striding towards her with a tall and lordly Arab one pace behind which turned Vivienne's knees to jelly.

Trent picked up her handbag. 'This is yours, I believe,' he said with dangerous calm.

'Th-thank you.' She felt as though she would shrivel under the blazing glitter in his eyes. He said something abruptly to Abdul who led the way in the gloom to where she soon saw, as Trent guided her with a vice-like grip on her elbow, the limousine was parked. It was obvious that the casino was close by and in her ignorance of its whereabouts she had run into him as he was leaving for the night. She cursed herself for her stupidity in not getting back to Koudia earlier. But there was nothing to be done about it now.

They made the journey back to the villa in silence, Abdul driving on the other side of the smoked glass screen, Trent seated beside her giving the impression of a rock about to split asunder. He was the first to alight from the car on the drive, and dispensing with Abdul with a brief goodnight he led her by the wrist into the house. Vivienne had never known such disciplined violence in a man and felt a little afraid as she tried to shake herself free at the foot of the stairs with the plea, 'It's late ... I'm very tired.' She felt a pain in her manacled wrist, and the breath was whipped from her throat as he jerked her under his luminous gaze and snapped, 'You weren't too tired to go wandering about the Medina. We'll talk. *Now.*'

He pushed her roughly before him towards the library and her anger mounting at the treatment she swung to face him blazingly as the door closed. He was more than a match for her indignation and fury, only his was the carefully controlled kind. He lit a cigarette as though to steady something slightly unbalanced inside him and spoke with a thin smile through the smoke. 'I always said you knew your way around, Vivienne. I'd like to bet this isn't the first time you've been out on your own.'

'No, it isn't.' She lifted her chin and flashed him a look. 'But I didn't know I had a keeper.'

'Are you suggesting it's *I* who sets a limit on your freedom?' There was a deadly silkiness in his tones before they exploded softly into something which shook their timbre. 'What about Rob? Doesn't he rate a little consideration?'

Vivienne felt a trembling inside her. She knew Trent's feelings where his brother was concerned. She was just as saddened and stricken as he was at Robert's declining health, but what could she do? What could either of them do? Unsteadily she retorted, 'That's unfair and you know it. I give all my time to Robert. What more can you expect?'

'Certainly, you give him your time. But maybe that's not quite how you planned your stay in Morocco—tied to an invalid chair.'

Vivienne forced herself to stay calm. What would Lucy have done in the circumstances? Dear Lucy, she would have spent the evenings lovingly stitching buttons on Robert's shirts and finding excuses to pop up to his room with books and warm drinks. But she wasn't Lucy. And she wasn't in love with Robert. She was fond of him, deeply so, but for her it was Gary ... Gary ... Gary.

She said levelly, 'I don't consider myself tied to Robert. We have tremendous fun through the day. You know yourself he needs a lot of rest.'

'It would give him a kick to know that you were somewhere close by, pulling for him,' Trent rasped with a sneer in his voice. 'I don't believe he has any idea that the streets of Tangier hold a bigger attraction. You must have got to know the town very well on your nightly jaunts.'

Facing him, Vivienne replied coldly, 'You're wrong if you think Tangier holds any special fascination for me. I go out ...' she shrugged, 'because it's something to do.'

'Of course,' he nodded, with his narrow-eyed gaze. 'You're young and healthy and you need excitement—the kind you don't find sitting in your room with a sick young man tucked away in some other part of the house.'

Vivienne's face drained of colour at the cheap significance of his remark. Her eyes flashing like molten amber, she took a step forward, but Trent was ready for her and grasped her by the shoulders as she might have struck him. In that powerful hold she could only murmur over her breathless anger, 'You don't have a very pretty mind, do you? Nor a very high opinion of me?'

'We're adults, you and I, Vivienne,' his curled smile was full of meaning. 'We know the ways of the world and what goes on between the people in it.' His fingers sank into her flesh through her thin blouse. She felt nailed by his blue gaze and saw as though for the first time the fleshless brown lines of his face and the unyielding force there. For a long moment she was speechless, then struggling in his grasp she said hotly, 'It's all very well for you. You have the casino to go to each evening. You don't have to stay in the house counting the hours till bedtime.'

'That's right, I don't,' he drawled with menacing calm. 'But I'm Rob's brother, not the girl he's crazily in love with.' His grip was suddenly bruising. 'How do you think he would feel if anything happened to you.'

'What *could* happen?' She defied him with her gaze. 'Tangier is a tourist city. It's perfectly safe to go out for a stroll in the evening.' Then remembering her mishap she added with a swift lowering of her dark lashes, 'Tonight was just an isolated incident. I was foolish enough to lose my way and asked for directions. I wasn't too upset about it.'

'Sure! You could have coped with those young thugs mauling you and trying to strip you of your belongings.' Vivienne winced. She had seen Trent in many moods, but savage and angry like this? She felt a little dazed.

Perhaps it was something in her half-closed eyes that made him relent and let go of her abruptly. He dragged on his cigarette for a full minute before saying brusquely and not without a trace of sarcasm, 'All right, let's think this thing out rationally. Maybe it is asking too much of you to sit tight in the house every night. If it makes you happier taking a walk, okay. But you don't go out alone. I'll get Abdul to drive you into town, and he can escort you wherever you want to go.'

Vivienne took care not to show any reaction, though her mind was working fast enough. How would she ever find Gary with Abdul tagging along? She replied coldly, 'I'm a grown woman, Trent. I don't need an Arab protector following in my footsteps every time I go out for a stroll.'

'Take it or leave it,' he said in clipped tones. 'The grounds are big enough for taking the night air. If you've got a hankering for the bright lights, then Abdul goes too. You're my responsibility with Rob the way he is.' He finished harshly, 'For his sake I intend to see that no harm comes to you.'

Vivienne knew there was no point in arguing, but something in her wouldn't let her acquiesce gracefully with this man. She tossed her head, the nostrils of her rather fine straight nose flaring a little as she purred, 'Maybe you've got used to running Rob's life. But don't try it with me, Trent. I like to make my own decisions.'

His hand came down on the knob of the door. Pausing before he opened it, his arm preventing her from leaving, he said suavely, 'While you're at Koudia you'll have to forgo that luxury. My only concern is that Rob gets a fair deal. You've got time to make it up to yourself later; he hasn't.' Flinty irony was in his gaze as it raked her tumbling hair and slightly dishevelled look, then he said, opening the door leisurely, 'If you're going to be up bright and early as usual in the morning, it might be an idea to catch up on a little beauty sleep.'

Out in the hall Vivienne answered his goodnight shortly and made straight for her room. There she paced the balcony until her breathing had subsided. It was true, she had almost bungled everything for Lucy tonight, but need Trent have been so overbearingly displeased about it? She had always felt that he would be a dangerous man to tangle with; now, rubbing her bruised shoulders, she knew that she had been right.

Vivienne slept late the next morning. She rose with a slightly guilty feeling and wanting to make it up to Lucy and to Robert, she showered and dressed with care. She found a daisy necklace for the round neck of her white tailored dress and clipped a matching daisy in each ear. Her hair, smoothed away from her temples, waved softly down to her shoulders and with a healthy bloom on her cheeks she congratulated herself that no one would suspect she had been up until after two last night.

Breakfast had already begun when she arrived at the pool. As she walked across to the raised terrace it was impossible not to feel a lightness in her step at the sheer brilliance of the day. The sun, already increasing in heat, caressed her bare arms, tanned to a warm gold now through so much outdoor living. Vivid magenta bougainvillea vied with the deep and endless blue of the sky for colour, next to the royal blue of irises, delicate delphiniums and the red and pink glow of geraniums. A posy of pastel-tinted freesias decorated the breakfast table.

Vivienne went up to Robert and dropped a kiss on his cheek, saying as blithely as she could, 'Sorry I'm late, folks. All this sunshine must be making me extra drowsy.'

'Hey, you should sleep in more often!' Mischievously Robert grabbed her and turning his cheek jerked her back to him. 'Do that again.'

Notching one up for Lucy, she kissed him unhurriedly and he in turn ran his fingers along her arm and brushed his lips playfully along the tip of her nose.

She took her seat at the table, her and Trent's gaze not quite meeting. He poured tea for her into a delicate china cup and she prattled gaily on about it being a gorgeous day and how the scent of orange blossom was intoxicating. He quipped lazily that it was probably the flower of the tangerine that was making her punch-drunk, and she knew that he approved of her mood for Robert's sake.

The young invalid had his own reasons for feeling breezy.

'Guess what?' he told her as soon as the meal was under way. 'Trent's got an idea for putting a croquet lawn on the spare patch at the side of the house.' He fiddled with his chopped grapefruit and shot her a facetious gleam. 'He thinks we haven't got enough to amuse you here at Koudia.'

Vivienne met Trent's gaze then and though their looks at each other spoke volumes she joked with oblique humour, 'Sounds like the right kind of sport for these pool layabouts. Swinging a mallet should make a change from ducking defenceless females!'

'That's what I thought,' Trent said with his tight grin, quick to take up the teasing with her. 'These guys have it all their own way in the water. A bit of skill in the way of a ball and a few hoops could be the answer to cutting them down to size.'

'Don't go kidding yourself that I'm new to the game,' Robert gave her a menacing smile, enjoying every minute of the ribbing. He flashed his brother a conspiratorial twinkle. 'Trent's seen me. There's a croquet pitch at the hospital. I've played a few games with the convalescents. Tell her, Trent.'

His brother confessed warningly with an amused glint, 'I have to admit he packs a mean mallet.'

Robert gave a satisfied grin. 'Croquet's not an old lady's pastime, you know. There's quite a few wheelchair champions.'

'Help!' Vivienne winced laughingly. 'I think I prefer the swimming pool!'

The banter continued throughout breakfast and long after the three of them had adjourned to the poolside, Vivienne put all she had into keeping the fun at top pitch. Trent joked as usual with his brother. Between them, she thought, they made a good team in creating a gay atmosphere. It didn't matter that she and Trent didn't get on; that behind their smiles was the fierce clash of personalities. Nothing mattered except Robert's happiness.

Work started on the croquet lawn the following morning. Berber labourers employed in the orchards came to transplant what they could of the ornamental bushes and level the land, and great lorry loads of smooth green turf were delivered. Vivienne watched the operations from her balcony with an acid smile. Trent had only to snap his fingers to get these jobs done. Running the casino took care of everything.

In less than a week the lawn was laid and ready for use. It was a good spot to idle away the sunny hours. It was on the plateau overlooking the bay, and therefore tempered by sea breezes yet near enough to the house to pop indoors when one wanted a breather. For the first few days the croquet pitch was a source of fascination to the servants. Everyone was fond of Robert and they all worked hard in their different ways to show no pity at his condition.

Momeen was the first to try his hand with the mallet. He tapped the ball as though he was lightly shelling an egg with a teaspoon, taking a dozen strokes to get to the nearest hoop, and Robert almost laughed himself out of his chair. Maurice came out, his hands full of flour, to give Vivienne a few pointers in the game. He had travelled extensively and he told her, his chef's hat slanting in a rakish manner, that in America they took the game of croquet very seriously. Haroun propelled Robert's wheelchair from hoop to hoop. It was agreed that the big Moor was best thus employed after he had swung the mallet like a sledgehammer thinking, with his big grin, that the idea was to try to hit the ball into the sea!

The days passed much the same as before, but with one difference. Trent had had the wine-coloured car overhauled and polished and he drove himself to the casino in the evenings. The black limousine waited on the drive each night, and Abdul was on hand indoors should he be needed. At first Vivienne had been too nervous to make a move from her room. Then she got to thinking that if she didn't go out at all Trent would think that she had something to hide. Besides, the urge in her was strong to continue her search for Gary. Sometimes she mused on her foolishness. After four years he could be married now with young children. Yet somehow she didn't think so. Hadn't he told her often enough during their summer together that he wasn't the marrying kind?

After a week she plucked up the courage to tell Abdul that she would be going out, soon after Trent had left for the casino one evening. She made herself ready in her room and came downstairs again to find the car engine turning over gently in the drive. Abdul was the one member of the staff she had never really got to know. He was Trent's right-hand man, and apart from meeting him in the house when he supervised the work-boys from the orchards who came to polish the floors, she had had little to do with him. How she was going to cope with him tagging around all evening she couldn't imagine.

He was holding the car door for her out on the drive. Used to speaking French and knowing that she was fluent in the language, he asked politely, once she was settled in her seat, 'What is Mademoiselle's choice?'

She hesitated, then spoke with a rush. 'I thought it might be interesting to stroll in the little *socco* near the Grand Mosque. There's a Moorish café there with Arab music and some of the shops might still be open.'

He bowed slightly and took his place behind the wheel, leaving her to the unnerving privacy of the rear compartment of the limousine as they glided away. He knew just where to park in town and waited discreetly in the background until she made up her mind which way to go. Oddly enough she soon got used to his presence a few steps behind her. In his smooth djellabah of tissue-fine linen, red fez, and heelless babouches of soft yellow leather, he made a commanding figure as he followed in her wake along the populated thoroughfares. And she had to admit he was useful in keeping the eternal supplicants who battened on to tourists at bay. Whining figures with hands outstretched, or clutching some gew-gaw for which they demanded a laughable sum, were exterminated like vermin by his sharp black-eyed gaze, and his biting stream of Arabic. Yet later when he ordered mint tea for her in the Moorish café, he smiled at her with his eyes in that remote, aloof way of his, and she saw all the pride of Arab stock in his saturnine, hawklike face.

Of course she kept her eyes peeled for Gary the whole of the time, but with Abdul attached to her like a limpet, her movements were hampered. The Arab manservant had his orders from Trent and even if she had run into a long-lost friend she doubted whether she would get as far as a handshake before he distrustfully stepped in wielding the little jewelled dagger he carried.

However, he had no idea what she had on her mind and after a night or two of his company she began to wonder if it would do any harm to make a few discreet enquiries. She was amazed how easy it was when she tried it. She suggested a stroll along the Boulevard Pasteur and on the pretext of feeling like some refreshment dropped into the bar lounge of the Hotel Riadh. Later while Abdul paced in his soft-shoed way in the foyer she spoke a few low words with the receptionist at the desk. Yes, he remembered Gary playing in the hotel dance band. He hadn't seen or heard of him for some time. All he could tell her was that he believed the man she was looking for had found employment after leaving the hotel in a small nightclub down by the port.

Vivienne walked along the boulevard, elated. She had actually talked with someone who knew Gary. It could now only be a matter of time before she traced him. Another night she went down to the *bar de nuit* the receptionist had mentioned and found it a seedy little club, reeking with an odour of stale drink and Turkish cigarettes. They remembered Gary. He had played there on and off on the rickety little dais where a blues pianist now stroked the keys in a melancholy stupor. But nobody knew where he was now. They could give her an old address of his. She accepted discreetly and hurried away, trying to give the impression, as far as Abdul was concerned, of having chosen badly in an attempt to review the night spots.

And so she went on, following up the leads on Gary. At first she was blissfully optimistic as so many people remembered him and this was an improvement on just raking the faces of the passers-by, but as the clues thinned out and each one led her to a dead end she was hit by a feeling of despondency. One evening she arrived back at Koudia a little after midnight and after thanking Abdul went to her room and flopped in an armchair. She had combed the city of Tangier, the old and the new town. There was just nowhere else to look.

She viewed the twinkling panorama from the balcony doorway. Could she resign herself to the fact that she would never see Gary again? Even though he might be one of those teeming millions down there? She rose slackly and wandered to the outdoors. She would have to. She had run out of ideas.

And it wasn't just that. As she cast her glance over the dark, silent house, and strained her ears for sounds of a car coming along the orchard road, another worry was beginning to make itself felt. How near had she come to giving herself away in her reckless search for Gary? It was true she had taken all possible precautions when making enquiries about him, but supposing Abdul wasn't as remote and detached as he appeared? And supposing he gossiped like any other manservant when he was alone with his master?

A tiny pulse began to throb in her temple. Her behaviour, now, looked a little foolish and she was tormented with one nagging little doubt. How much did Trent suspect?

CHAPTER FOUR

THURSDAY was Robert's day for the hospital. How much he guessed of the discord between her and Trent, Vivienne didn't know, but he made a surprise suggestion while they were leisurely taking breakfast that morning.

'Know what I've been thinking?' The sun set alight the blond hair framing his tanned, handsome face and boyish grin as he cast a slightly anxious glance in his brother's direction. 'It's an awful waste of a day, Viv, hanging around the house while I'm away. Why don't you take her out somewhere, Trent? The two of you can drop me off at the hospital and call for me around six tonight.'

Trent's expression changed in no way. He said lazily, replacing the sugar bowl, 'That would be for Vivienne to decide, Rob. I don't know how she'd feel about taking a trip out with me.'

'Well, ask her.' Exasperation in his grin, he turned his anxiety her way and waited.

Trent said casually, 'How about it, Vivienne? Shall we do as Rob says and join forces in a little relaxation?'

Vivienne's heart had started on a wild tattoo. A whole day with Trent! The idea both appalled and fascinated her. She refused to be afraid of him and this seemed as good a way as any of showing it. And what would she have to worry about with no talk of Lucy's letters to trip her up? 'I do get to feel a bit at a loose end here on my own.' She looked at Robert rather than Trent as she spoke, and smiled, 'How nice of you to suggest it.'

'You deserve it.' Robert reached out and took one of her hands in his, smiling too in a lopsided, grateful way. 'A break from Koudia—and me—will do you good.'

Vivienne kept her lashes lowered. He knew nothing of her nocturnal outings to the city. But Trent did, and for this reason she battled to keep the colour from her cheeks and studiously avoided his gaze.

Later, upstairs in her room, she wondered what on earth had possessed her to agree to suffer the company of the tyrant older brother for several hours. And yet there was something of a challenge in accepting, so much so that to back out now, to send word downstairs that she had changed her mind, seemed a very dull alternative. She laid out a summer dress of blue flowered nylon. Though she couldn't have explained why, she took more than usual care with her toilette.

Abdul drove them to the hospital. Haroun took his day off on Thursdays and they dropped him off at the Café Central in town. There was amused speculation inside the car as to how the big Moor would spend his time in this fashionable rendezvous for Europeans, knowing as he did very little French or English.

'Where he's going communication is unimportant, except with the stomach,' Trent said with a knowing gleam. 'I bet he'll head for the Parade restaurant in the Rue Goya. They've got a Belgian chef there who makes cous-cous like he never tasted in Marrakesh.'

'Perhaps he just enjoys the tourist atmosphere,' Vivienne suggested with a smile.

Robert shook his head and grinned. 'It's all a blind. As soon as we've disappeared he'll cut through into the Medina. From what I can understand of his Arab jokes I'd say he knows his way around with the women there.'

The genial athlete with the big brown biceps gave his usual *Insh'-Allah* salute and moved off, taking his secret with him.

Vivienne stayed in the car outside the hospital. Trent and Abdul got Robert into the wheelchair and manoeuvred him up the shallow flight of steps at the main entrance. They were met there by two distinguished-looking figures in white coats whom she took to be Robert's doctors. After a brief conversation they all went indoors. For a while she passed the time admiring the smooth lawns and neat flower

beds in the hospital grounds. When the waiting became a
little tedious she got out and strolled to where a slight
knoll looked on to a grove of olive and palm trees. She
was making the most of the breeze coming over the rise
when Trent returned. He offered her a hand to make it
down the slope, the flimsiness of her dress blowing against
him as he helped her. He said with an impersonal smile,
'Sorry you had to wait, but the doctors kept me longer
than usual this morning.'

On the flat she shot him a quick worried glance. Was it
to do with Robert? Was that what had taken so long? His
face told her nothing. Searching it as he guided her to the
car, she hadn't the courage to ask. Beside her, he said, once
they were in motion again, 'It's market day in the Grand
Socco. Abdul can drop us off there. This afternoon we
could take a run out to Tetuan. If the idea appeals?'

'Sounds fine,' Vivienne replied, adopting a distant tone.
All at once she was struck with a feeling of regret that there
could be no real camaraderie between them. She dared not
risk being just herself when there was Robert and Lucy to
consider. And Trent had always been distrustful of her.
Strangely enough none of this showed when later they
made their way up the teeming street and through the Bab
el Fahs gateway that led to the Grand Socco. She couldn't
help noticing the kind of exclusive quality he possessed as
they mingled with the crowd, both occidental and oriental.
There was nothing exceptional about his clothes. He wore a
pair of pale slacks and a sky-blue shirt, and he moved with
an easy, withdrawn attitude. Yet there was something in his
manner, in the strong, lean lines of his profile, that made
him stand out from the rest.

With a hand on her elbow he guided her into the busy,
bustling atmosphere of the market place, where they
browsed among Safi pottery, basket work, handwoven
lengths of cloth and all kinds of Eastern bric-à-brac. But
it was the flower section in the open air bazaar which
attracted Vivienne. She liked to watch the colourful Riff
women in their red and white striped skirts and enormous

straw hats decorated with pompoms, arranging the great load of blooms they had brought down from the mountains. Under the trees they sat surrounded by roses, gladioli, ixias and a host of other varieties, making a galaxy of colour. The most popular of all was the exquisite blue flower of which there were many in the garden of Koudia, the famous Moroccan iris.

Trent accompanied her with an air of lazy tolerance, and she almost forgot the rift that lay between them as he made dry comments on the alarming profusion of Oriental junk on the stalls, and handled with her weird skins, stringed instruments and old brass-studded leather caskets. By the time they had got down to the foot of the *socco* where more Moorish wares were on sale in the booths lining the street Vivienne felt laughter bubbling in her throat and a curious feeling of release from all the inhibitions that dogged her.

It was perhaps a dangerous mood in which to stop, as she did at a spot festooned with a grotesque assortment of dead birds, animal skins, dried snakes and lizards. 'It's a medicine shop!' she exclaimed laughing-eyed, and pushed the strands of hair back from her face with an unconscious gesture. 'It's incredible to think that they still believe in these kind of cures in this day and age.'

'You'd be surprised,' Trent nodded with a grin. 'Out here magic possets and mysterious powders still hold great sway with the population.'

While they were talking the owner of the shop thrust his bearded head out of the doorway. 'You would like a potion?' he asked in passable English.

'Not right now,' Trent gleamed. 'We were just wondering about the use of these things.'

The owner, who introduced himself as the great doctor Moulay Ahmed, eyed them with a polite and sympathetic beam as he spoke. 'I am sure you will need something. But first if you wish I will explain a little of my business. This dried eagle has a very important use. If someone puts a love potion in your tea a little of the dried flesh, powdered and drunk in water, will break the spell. These fox bones are for a love potion. Ground and blended with this powdered lizard skin, they are irresistible, also very cheap. Now if another man is courting your sweetheart and you wish . . .'

Vivienne, listening with a smile, felt that the ground had suddenly disappeared from under her feet. But Trent was interjecting easily, 'Just a minute. Don't you have anything else to cure but lovesickness around here?'

Ahmed smiled with leering innocence. 'But of course,' he said. 'When a man comes to my shop with a woman, naturally I draw conclusions. Now on that hook there is a bit of desert wolfskin. If you have an infection just drop the skin in the fire and hold the infected part in the smoke. And this snakeskin—it is a genuine Taroudannt cobra, no less—you can rent by the day. Wrap it around your brow if you have a headache. For a sore throat, wear it like a scarf. It is very powerful.'

'I bet,' Trent murmured humorously, and dropping an arm negligently around Vivienne's shoulders he eased himself away. 'Well, thanks for the run-down, Ahmed. Now we must be cutting along.'

'Wait a minute!' As they were passing the baskets of dried lizards Ahmed called out, 'How many children have you?'

While Vivienne wished now that the ground would indeed open and swallow her up Trent replied lazily that they didn't have any.

'Aha!' Ahmed exclaimed. 'Then you need me. Now this dried leopard . . .'

'Let's get out of here!' They were well away from the booth-lined street before Trent's throaty laughter subsided. Vivienne felt a little breathless. She was glad that they turned into the shady calm of the Mendoubia Gardens, where only the centuries-old trees were witness to her slightly pink cheeks.

They lunched at the Thousand and One, where the atmosphere was truly reminiscent of the Arabian Nights. Though none of it was new to Vivienne she was aware more than she had ever been of the magic of their surroundings, in Trent's company; aware of the Moorish dishes prepared by a Moorish cook, of the orchestra playing Moorish music and the dancing of the boys which carried one back to the dawn of civilisation. The Menebhi Palace was close by and their table had a view of the sea. There was a piquancy about everything which could have been simply the brilliant sunshine and azure blue sky.

They left to join the passing parade in the alleys. When they got back to the spot where they had been dropped off earlier that morning Vivienne was pleasantly surprised to see the wine-coloured sports car waiting by the curb. She said laughingly, for it was that kind of day, 'So we're not to have a chauffeur for our afternoon drive?'

'Sure we have a chauffeur—me,' Trent joked idly, putting her into the passenger seat. He came round to slide in beside her and added casually, with a grin, 'Abdul's okay for browsing around town, but out on the highway he'll handle the car like a string of camels and we could end up riding into the sunset in the Goulimine desert.' He was still joking, of course. Vivienne had a feeling that Abdul, though absent, was completely reliable.

The car ate up the kilometres out of the city. The breeze wafting over the windscreen was perfumed by oleander blossoms growing in bright pink clumps on the banks of the streams by the roadside. Vivienne was in the mood for chat, but it was awkward with Trent. They had no common ground on which to base a conversation. Over lunch they had centred their talk on the food, the music and the view. Now because she could think of nothing else to say she asked lightly, 'Is Abdul married?'

'I believe he's got one or two wives tucked away somewhere in the south at Zagora,' Trent replied. He turned the wheel round a bend and shot her a laconic look. 'But don't run away with the idea that he's lonely in Tangier. Like Haroun, he's got his special lady friends in the medina.'

Vivienne eyed his half-smile and twinkled accusingly, 'You talk as if you condone that kind of thing. Wouldn't it be better if you had his wives brought to Koudia, then he could live in an aura of respectability?'

Trent laughed, showing strong white teeth. 'I doubt if we'd get that. It would be a battle between the house and the Medina with the women on both sides concocting their powerful *chu-bas*. You can take it from me they'd have far more potency than anything Moulay Ahmed showed us today. Poor Abdul wouldn't stand a chance.'

'It would serve him right if he were laid low with a posset,' Vivienne said with stern satisfaction. 'It would teach him to take his marriages seriously.' She cast a sideways glance at Trent's bland exterior and smiled hypocritically, 'I somehow get the feeling you don't agree.'

He shrugged, his blue gleam aimed at the road. 'Man is polygamous by nature. The East recognises that. We in the West try to make out it's primitive, but there's an awful lot of envy goes on.'

'Among the men, naturally,' Vivienne purred. Somehow the subject and Trent's attitude nettled her. She changed it, stifling a slightly morose feeling, by remarking, 'Zagora is a long way from here, almost on the southern borders of Morocco.'

Trent nodded. 'That's where Abdul and I first met up. He was employed then by a mate of mine, a veteran of the French camel patrol. Then Pierre went back to France, so Abdul came to work for me.'

'The French camel patrol?' Vivienne looked at Trent, intrigued. 'You mean wandering among the nomadic tribes and camping in those red mud forts set in the middle of the desert like something straight out of *Beau Geste*?' At his nod she pushed a strand of hair from her face and enquired, 'What were you doing in a place like that?'

'Something along the same lines.' After several moments had elapsed he shot a grin her way and asked, 'What's wrong? Can't you picture me pouring sand out of my boots?'

'As you are now, maybe,' she viewed him in his casual wear, 'but in the evenings when you're dressed for the casino I wouldn't have connected you with anything so adventurous.'

His grin broadened. 'Don't let the city folk fool you. I've lived in some rough places.'

Vivienne turned her glance to the scenery and mused on what she had just learned. So Trent had another side to his character; one where he had been accustomed to roving as he pleased in raw and unpopulated spots. It was certainly a contrast to the groomed and polished life he led now, and it set her thinking. Which, she wondered, was the real Trent? It was an interesting question.

The landscape was un-African to look at. Cows grazed in the meadows and trees covered the hillsides. There were birds everywhere, small woodpeckers, partridges, and swallows, and in the hedgerows an endless variety of wild flowers. Then suddenly they were twisting down a steep red clay road, the hills fell away and they entered the narrow streets of Tetuan.

It was pleasant wandering in the Andalusian atmosphere of the old Spanish quarter. They took tea at one of the sidewalk cafés and later strolled through the Moorish section, whose winding streets gave glimpses of the mountains. Beyond the Bab Rouah gateway they were caught in the market place again. Here richly embroidered cloths, woven belts and silver jewellery winked in the sunlight. Here too were the inevitable booths displaying the usual bizarre merchandise. Without thinking Vivienne took Trent's arm and guided him away from where snakeskins and dried animal pelts adorned a doorway, stating humorously, 'I think one medicine shop will suffice for today.'

His blue gaze fencing teasingly with hers, he drawled, 'Not interested in hearing what's all the rage in the Tetuan love potion racket?' They laughed together and somehow ended up walking hand in hand. They studied the alleyways of the Medina from a point high up in the Casbah, and the forest of minarets, cheerfully counting no less than seventy in the town. Beyond was the Mediterranean, a deep royal blue, and in the distance it was possible to see the coast of Spain in the clear light, and the little white town of Tarifa.

Vivienne found a seat on the rough Casbah wall and put her face to the breeze laced with multitudinous scents from the streets below. Eyes closed, she was trying to place some of them—fresh fish grilled on charcoal, simmering tajine stew—when she felt Trent at her side. He offered her a cigarette, flicked his lighter under it and the one he had placed between his own lips and after inhaling said with his idly probing expression, 'For someone who's only been here a short time you're pretty blasé about your surroundings.'

So he had noticed that nothing caused her any great surprise. She smiled and replied lightly, 'There's a simple explanation—I've been to Morocco before.'

He looked in no way shaken by her remark but merely commented, 'For a farmer's daughter you get around.'

Vivienne slid her glance towards the sea. She didn't want to think of Lucy. Not just now. She reflected dreamily, 'I can remember the way Fez used to look, rose-pink in the moonlight, and how the fort and mosque on the hillside at el Jadida shone brilliant white against the blue sky.'

'How long ago was that?' He rested a well shod foot on the low wall beside her.

'Four years.' Where was Trent then, she wondered, jogging into an oasis on camelback? Or preparing to explore the bright lights in some north African city?

He was asking, 'And you never had a hankering to make a return visit?'

'No,' she replied non-committally.

'Strange! They say Morocco is more Eastern than the East. I'd have thought you'd have been bitten if only in a mild way by——' he shrugged with a lazy grin, 'well, whatever it is that gets one about these places.'

'Perhaps I was. I came back, didn't I?' Her smile held, but only just. There they were brushing close to *that* subject again.

Trent lowered his gaze fractionally too. He took a pull

on his cigarette, then lapsed into a reflective mood himself. 'I remember when I first saw you at the airport that day,' he looked down at her with ironic humour. 'I had an idea then that you didn't exactly regard Tangier as the wilds of Africa. You had a look that froze the touts. I think you would have managed to shake them off without any help from me.'

'True.' Vivienne bowed low at this touch of flattery. She took advantage of the situation to add boldly, 'I would have handled the boys in the Medina too if you hadn't have happened along.'

'Young thugs, and not all of them boys.' Trent's attitude became steely. 'That was a different matter.'

'Not so very, for me,' Vivienne shrugged. 'I got to know the streets of Tangier very well and learned a lot about Moroccan youths during my six months' stay here.'

The look he gave her was long and searching. He said at last, with a quixotic gleam, 'You're a mysterious creature. I've always felt there was something about you that doesn't add up. What happened here four years ago?'

Vivienne felt a jolt inside. Had she gone too far rambling on about herself? Adopting an air of flippancy, she said laughingly, 'Does something have to have happened simply because I got a fancy to do a little travelling?'

But Trent didn't let up on his scrutiny. He said, smiling too in an odd way, 'You're old enough to have had half a dozen love affairs.'

The laughter came through her parted lips as she looked up at him and she felt her breath stop in her throat. She managed to retort humorously, 'Well, for my tender age, where does that put you?'

'For a man it's different. We're not inclined to carry the scars like you women.'

In the face of his male superiority she was fired into flashing back, albeit sweetly, 'In everything men give so little of themselves.'

'I wouldn't say that,' he drawled, his blue gaze on her. 'It depends.'

She felt trapped by his stifling proximity, but by no means helpless—at least not too much that she couldn't breathlessly twinkle a reply. 'I do remember you saying when we first met that you never made love by proxy.'

'Nor would you be satisfied with that either. I said that too.'

Up until this moment she hadn't wanted to be reminded of Lucy and the business of the letters. Now, like someone drowning, she clutched at the one subject that could save her. 'I'm lucky.' It was all she could do to keep her voice light. 'I was able to meet my pen-pal beau in the flesh.'

'Are you?' There was a wealth of meaning and scepticism in his tones. His blue gaze still held hers, but she knew that the spell was broken. After a moment he tossed his cigarette over the wall and they watched it roll and spark in the breeze down the cobbled ramp that led below. He straightened, thrust his hands in his pockets and spoke to the minaret skyline. 'Four years ago, Rob was a healthy young cuss. His one ambition was to become a professional rugby player. He had the build for it.'

'He still has a wonderful physique,' Vivienne said, smiling.

'Not as he was in those days.' Trent's gaze narrowed over the view. 'He was a young giant. He could tackle anybody on the field.'

'Did he get to play professionally?' Vivienne finished her cigarette.

'More than that. His room's full of trophies. He was touring up to about a year ago. Then this muscular thing hit him.'

'It must have been something of a shock,' Vivienne put in.

'No, nothing like that. It didn't happen that fast. At first they thought it was just an attack of 'flu. Then he didn't pick up ...' Trent turned his glance, somewhat sceptically her way. 'But no doubt Rob's told you all this in his letters?'

'Oh, of course!' Vivienne hurried to reply. 'It's ... just

nice to hear it from an older brother.'

She had risen to give some credence to her words. Trent was facing her now. His gaze roamed over her windblown features, then he smiled, but spoke harshly. 'Sure. An older brother can be a comfort at times.'

The lighter mood of earlier had evaporated. Talking of Rob had put a sombre feel over everything. Trent looked at his watch and taking her arm he said abruptly, 'It's time we were getting back to the hospital.'

They didn't speak during the return journey to Tangier. Robert, looking paler as though his day at the hospital had tired him a little, was nevertheless in cheerful frame of mind. 'Well, how'd it go, folks?' he asked as soon as they had got him settled in the car and were driving back to Koudia. 'Did you have a good day?'

'Splendid,' said Trent, his eyes on the road.

'Wonderful!' Vivienne prattled. 'We toured the market this morning, then we had lunch at the Thousand and One, and later we drove over to Tetuan.'

'Good!' said Robert, looking first at her and then at Trent. 'I like to think that my best girl and my brother can rub along okay together. You must do it again.'

Trent swung the wheel and drawled, 'Don't forget I've a business to run, Rob. I've never yet met an accountant who can do the figures my way.'

Vivienne said, looking out of the window, 'I should really have written some letters home today,' and then to change the subject she pointed as they drove through the orchards. 'Oh, look! The blossom has made a lovely pink carpet under the trees. I bet it smells delicious.'

But there was no doubt that she and Trent were back on their respective sides of the fence and for the rest of that week they spoke little to one another. Trent avoided her, she thought, except at the meal tables and the afternoons beside the pool. She told herself that that was fine by her; they really had very little in common. She even welcomed the old antagonism that came bubbling to the surface every time she thought of him. What did she know about casinos except that it was an occupation and a way of making money that she abhorred?

Of course there was no tangible rift between them. On the face of it nothing had changed. Trent was his usual suave self in front of Robert. He made jokes at the table and beside the pool. Only Vivienne could feel the steely detachment in him where she was concerned. As it happened she had other things to occupy her mind.

Robert was becoming increasingly dependent on her company throughout the day. They spent long sessions together in the garden grounds of Koudia. Wheelchair-ridden as he was, he had grown close to and developed a deep love for nature, noticing things around him that he had never known existed in his hectic days as a rugby player. And from this love had stemmed an avid interest in the poets who had set nature to music in their words.

Vivienne had always known this from his letters and the endless quotations he had penned to Lucy and sometimes she would feel desperately inadequate when trying to supply some rapport to his moods. Sitting beside his chair on the mosaic-tiled seat one day, he said dreamily to her as he gazed at the sea and the low-lying hills across the bay, 'You know, it's funny, but I've never been on an island. I've seen the sea—quite a lot of different ones, in fact—but I've never known what it's like to have it all around me.'

'England's an island,' Vivienne quipped. And then thoughtfully, 'But I know what you mean. I went to the Isle of Man once. If anything I'd say it gives one a feeling of loneliness.'

'You could be right,' Robert nodded, still smiling absently into the distance.

Vivienne was thinking privately of the tragedy of it. Only twenty-four. And he would never see an island now. She eyed his fine straw-blond head, thick brown neck and powerful shoulders and wept a little inwardly as she often did at this sad waste of young manhood. Then he startled her by reciting, as though his mind was still out there somewhere afar, *'Willows whiten, aspens quiver, little breezes dusk and shiver Through the wave that runs for-ever By the island in the river ...'*

Lucy would have known how to reply. A plain girl, but gentle and sincere, she too had this affinity with nature and love of the poets. Didn't most of her letters to Robert con-tain, with shy simplicity, the answering half to one of his penned quotations? But because she, Vivienne, was at a loss in this wonderland of prose she said laughingly, 'What's that? It sounds eerie.'

Robert came back from the distance as though the mood had been lost. She sensed that he felt let down at her lack of response, although he explained cheerfully enough, 'It's the island of Shalott. I suppose it is eerie in a way. The lady of Shalott was cursed, but she saw her knight, so she found a boat and left the island anyway.' He said dramatically, *'She loosed the chain and down she lay. The broad stream bore her far away ...'*

'Good! So she was no longer lonely.' Vivienne stood up. Out of her depth as she was, she couldn't wait to change the subject.

'More so than ever,' Robert grinned. 'She floated after her knight—*till her blood was frozen slowly and her eyes were darkened wholly*——' He gripped Vivienne's hands suddenly and eagerly and murmured, 'But your blood's not frozen. You're warm and lovely. Kiss me, Viv ...' He pulled her against him until she could feel the hard, muscu-lar force of his body. His mouth searched hungrily for hers and she gave it as she always did over the knot of distaste inside her for this trickery she was involved in. And it wasn't just that. In his arms as she often was these days she sensed an urgency in him, a need which frightened her because she had no idea how to deal with it.

When they returned to the poolside after these rather turbulent outings Trent would barely glance up from the table where he was working. He always appeared to be busy checking over the casino figures and wore a shut-down look of concentration. Despite his reserve where she was con-cerned Vivienne felt more at ease beside the pool. Robert's amorous advances were proving more and more difficult to cope with, and whereas she would at one time have baulked at Trent's company she found in it now a scant kind of comfort.

Besides, Robert loved the water, and swimming and splashing about he was less inclined to mischief. To offset any kind of disappointment he might feel in her behaviour when they were alone she went all out to make it up to him during their play sessions at the pool. Perhaps she took her enthusiasm a little too far, but the afternoon when she decided to present a rather more glamorous picture she was thinking only of pleasing Robert.

Instead of donning her swimsuit as she always did she searched out the bikini that Lucy had packed with it. It was of amber silk, and when she walked before the mirror in it she thought it gave her a girlish elegance. Her legs were long enough not to have to worry about wearing flat beach mules, and throwing a towelling robe over her arm she went downstairs. It didn't take her long to discover that her outfit was a success. Robert let out a long wolf whistle when he saw her. She had to walk down the length of the pool to his delighted whoops and cat-calls. But she pretended nonchalance and on her arrival she looked down at her body and lamented laughingly, 'The suit's all right, but what about the pale patches? I'll have to start sunbathing all over again.'

'That's not a bad idea,' Robert said with an artful grin. 'Pass me the lotion and I'll see that you're well covered.'

Vivienne had let herself in for that one, and as there was no way round it she gaily agreed. Standing there with Robert smoothing the liquid over her torso she didn't look Trent's way. As she had walked down the length of the pool she had tried not to think of him. She was only interested in playing a convincing part for Robert. He lingered over the job of basting her and while she lay in the hot sun he tickled her back with a palm frond unmercifully so that in the end she had to consent to joining him in the pool.

He no longer worried about her seeing Haroun carry him

to the water. This was perhaps because the big Moor had the sense to make a game of it. Indeed, athletic and beaming with energy, he was quick to join in the fun around the pool and the three of them had long ago become a team. Vivienne and Robert had picked up enough Arabic to communicate with their bronzed oversized playmate and this afternoon the gardens echoed with their shouts as they teased him with his own expressions. '*Wakhkha!*' Robert snorted, going like a steamboat and then coming up for air.

'*Walu!*' Vivienne sank theatrically beneath one of the floating armchairs.

Padding round the edge of the pool, stripped to the waist and prepared if necessary to scoop up his young charge with one hand, Haroun retaliated by rolling back on his heels and laughing jeeringly, '*El hamdu l-llah!*' Oho! He begins to get the hang of it! Or swelling up his powerful chest and biceps and strutting like an amiable King Kong, '*Ma shufti shay!*' Just wait—you haven't seen a thing yet!

Vivienne was weak with laughter. It *was* funny to see the big Moor in his cream cricket trousers and floppy turban ballet-dancing around the edge of the pool. When they were all worn out he brought drinks to the waterside. Vivienne stretched out on a floating lilo with hers. She wanted to tan her torso to the pale gold of the rest of her body and she spread herself luxuriating in the warmth of the sun.

Robert tired easier these days and she wasn't surprised when he told her a little later that he was going up to his room. In his wheelchair he lifted his face for her kiss and she watched him go, glad that they had had a wonderful afternoon together. There was a long gap between now and dinner, and as she often did at this hour she slipped on her robe and went for a stroll beyond the high hedge. It was her way of escaping for a little while from the crushing responsibilities thrust upon her. But this afternoon she wasn't to have even that respite.

Trent had walked back to the house alongside Robert, saying his goodnights and checking as he always did with

Haroun that his brother's meals and comforts were all taken
care of. Vivienne was a little startled therefore when only a
moment or two later he reappeared and followed her
through the gap in the hedge. His features were grim and
something told her that the occasion was hardly a social one,
although he strolled with her for a while, pointing out the
more exotic of the flowers and shrubs fast approaching the
full bloom of summer.

The afternoon was still hot. Trent wore cotton drill
slacks and a tailored sports shirt of strong brown mottled
tints which gave him an outdoor, virile look. They stopped
in the shade of a palm where a triangular view of the
orchards showed the myriad lines of young trees hung
with the green baubles of growing fruit and feather-fine
leaves. He spoke then, a little laconically, his gaze on the
view. 'You were saying you'd been to Tangier before. I
suppose you got to know your way around on the beaches
that summer?'

Though she was already attuned to his churlish mood
there was something in his tones that irked her. She replied
shortly, 'I was quite a sun-worshipper, if that's what you
mean. Is there something wrong in that?'

'Not when you go around decently dressed.' He turned
then and flicked a glance down the open front of her beach
robe. 'But maybe you find the habit of wearing little more
than a couple of stitches hard to break?'

So that was it! Quivering yet hardly knowing why, she
spoke up. 'If the bikini annoys you why not come out with
it and say so? I thought the idea was to keep Robert
happy?'

Trent said with clamped jaw, 'You don't have to hand it
to him on a plate.'

To Vivienne it seemed that the flush started somewhere
near her smooth midriff and rose slowly, painfully and
heatedly. Hardly caring now about her open robe, she
flung at him, 'You like to cheapen everything I do, don't
you? It doesn't matter to you that I've used nothing but a
one-piece bathing suit until today. I made the change for

Robert's sake, but it seems I can't win. Not long ago you were throwing him at me—physically. Now you're telling me I shouldn't wear a perfectly adequate bikini.'

'Adequate! That's a matter of opinion.' With a distorted smile his eyes raked her smooth brown flesh, then swung away. 'And it's not just Rob,' he said abruptly. 'In the privacy of one's own family this kind of thing is accepted. But there's Haroun to consider. How do you think he feels with you sporting yourself like a water nymph under his nose?'

'Haroun?' Vivienne stared. The big easy-going Moor took no more notice of her than if she had been a fish swimming about. She said with a half-laugh, 'Haroun isn't interested in the insipid white flesh of the West. I'd have to be a fat, shrouded figure in a *haik* before he'd even look at me.'

'They're all interested,' Trent said with a sneer. 'Don't let the veneer of indifference fool you. I'm a man, I should know.'

'Are you?' She gave him a look. 'I thought the only figures you were interested in were those to do with your profits at the casino?' She didn't know what had got into her, making such a remark, but it gave her a warm, animal-like satisfaction to see that it had gone home. Trent's face inclined to paleness just now, showed a dark suffusion of colour. His blue gaze, though resembling ice, glinted dangerously and as he looked her over he said lazily, 'That shows how little you know me, Vivienne. For your own good I suggest you take yourself off to your room and get into a little more clothing.'

'Don't worry, I'm going.' Angrily she belted up her robe. 'I've already got the message that I'm supposed to be some kind of Jezebel just because I chose to wear a different swimsuit. Well, I've got news for you.' She turned back with a parting shot. 'I'll wear my one-piece now till it drops in shreds—and it's well on the way.'

'I'll order a dozen more,' Trent snapped. 'That way there'll be no burst blood vessels.'

'Money is your answer to everything, isn't it?' she flung at him, moving off.

'Can you think of anything better?' he threw back.

'Give me time and I will.' Shakily she left him and hurried towards the house. By the time she had reached her room her heart was thudding and there was the bright glisten of tears in her eyes. She flung herself on the bed and sighed shudderingly. Why did they take so much out of her, these tiffs with Trent?

CHAPTER FIVE

DINNER was a strain that evening. Vivienne wished she had had the nerve to stay in her room. But that would have been bowing down to Trent's autocracy. Besides, she derived a certain masochistic pleasure in sharing his company for an hour. It was a kind of self-torture that she had never yet been willing to forgo.

She wondered sometimes if they were both taut and edgy with one another because of Robert. Though she hadn't wanted to admit it, even to herself, she had noticed his increasing pallor and flagging energy these past days. For some time now his complexion had been turning a putty colour, and his young face was developing a sunken look. Terror seized her whenever she thought of this insidious change in his appearance, and often she asked herself, was Trent watching and waiting too.

It was the day after his brother's weekly visit to the hospital that it happened, the moment she had dreaded. All the previous day while Robert was out she had kept to herself in the grounds. Trent had done likewise in the house. They had met only for meals when most of the chat was taken care of by Momeen, who always prattled away in French regardless of the atmosphere. There was none of the comparative gaiety of the week before when they had visited the market place and driven to Tetuan. Trent didn't come near the pool. Vivienne wandered round the ruined *minzah* beyond the mimosa thicket.

It was almost a relief to have Robert back the next day. Soon after breakfast he was eager to take their walk. Vivienne pushed his chair along the paths until they had the Casbah rooftops and the sweep of blue bay below them. The view always brought a look of extreme peace to his face. She sat beside him and they talked companionably, mainly hazarding guesses at the destinations of the ships in the harbour. But Robert obviously had other things on his mind. He took her hand at one point and said in those urgent tones, 'Viv, if only you and I could be like other couples. We could travel, see the world together. Book a double bunk in one of those tubs down there.'

Deliberately misinterpreting his grin, she said brightly, 'Well, for the moment we're not doing so badly. Here we are with a scintillating view ...'

'You know what I mean, Viv.' Robert wasn't to be side-tracked. There was hunger mingling with the humour in his gaze as he pulled her towards him. 'I want you close to me. I want to feel you in my arms ... If only I wasn't chained to this damned chair!' As he strained towards her she was inwardly horrified to see him almost make it on to the seat beside her. Then while she was wondering only how best not to hurt him, he gave a gasp and slumped forward.

It was fully a minute after she had watched him roll out of the chair and sprawl awkwardly on the path before her shocked senses recovered sufficiently for her to move. Then she ran, a strangled scream escaping from her throat. She didn't know that she was screaming for Trent. All she remembered was running ... running along the paths towards the house. She collided with him as he came from the direction of the pool, through the opening in the hedge.

There was no time to avoid his arms. He caught her to him and shakily, her face wet with tears, she blurted out what had happened. He turned an ashen colour when he heard, though his hold on her was steadying. Abdul, who was never far from his side, stepped forward. 'Take Miss Blyth to her room and get her a drink,' Trent said crisply. He gripped her for a moment encouragingly, then sprinted away through the grounds.

It was the longest morning Vivienne had ever lived through. White-faced, she watched the arrival of the doctors on the drive below, from the balcony outside her room. It seemed an eternity before they departed again. She paced the carpet until she thought she would collapse from nervous tension and anxiety. At last, unable to bear another moment not knowing, she had flung open the door and was about to go in search of news when Trent appeared.

Her terrified gaze searched his face. Amidst the weariness there she saw the glimmerings of a grin. He answered her unspoken question in a breath, 'He's okay.'

Vivienne slumped with relief. Trent led her to a tapestry-covered ottoman in the carpeted corridor and went on, 'It was a temporary collapse. In a few days he'll be back in his wheelchair. He'll need taking care of for a while——'

'Let me do it,' Vivienne put in swiftly. 'Haroun's all right, but Robert will want someone of his own kind with him if he's got to stick in bed all the time.'

'If you feel up to it,' Trent said with a nod. 'He's been asking for you.' He got up. 'After lunch I'll take you up to his rooms.'

The afternoon sunlight was filtering under the shady archways fronting the house when he guided her down the long hall and into the left wing of the villa. A lift had been installed to accommodate Robert's wheelchair and they went up in this to the top suite. The rooms, Vivienne saw, were ideal for an invalid. Every window commanded a view of rolling countryside, city or sea, and the breeze wafting in was scented with the nearby cedars and pines.

Robert was sitting up in bed, in his bedroom, a manly clutter of books, models and gadgets around him. Supported by pillows and still alarmingly pale, he grinned weakly when he saw Vivienne. 'Hi! How was that for a fade-out? I hope I didn't scare you.'

'You did a little, but it doesn't matter. The main thing is, you're all right.'

'Doesn't matter! I'm as annoyed as hell.' He quirked a look at her and murmured with sly humour, 'Trust me to pass out just when we were getting to the interesting bit!'

Very much aware of Trent in the room, Vivienne said with pink cheeks, briskly straightening the bed, 'Well, that kind of mischief's finished with for the time being. Now you're going to have to put up with me dishing out your medicine and serving up your food, and it's no good pleading no appetite with me.'

Robert looked bemusedly from her to his brother and exclaimed, 'Hey, I've got my own nurse! Is that right, Trent? She's going to keep me company until I can get downstairs?'

'That's what she wants,' Trent said with his affectionate gleam. 'Haroun can do the heavy work. Vivienne will keep you posted as to what's going on in the rest of the house. I'll drop in from time to time.'

It was no easy task that Vivienne had set herself. Robert was very much dependent on help since his collapse and there were so many things to do to keep him happy and relaxed. She spent the mornings with him, left him for a couple of hours in the afternoon, when he had a nap, and read to him or played cards with him in the evening until Haroun settled him for the night. Sometimes she and Trent had dinner with him in his room. Momeen would come up and with great ceremony lay the long table under the window. Expensive linen, silver and crystalware were trundled up in the lift and Maurice the chef used his imagination, arranging tempting displays and scribbling little messages with his icing squeezer on the tops of Robert's favourite delicacies.

The table, softly lit with candelabra and overlooking the winking lights of the city, looked inviting indeed. There was nothing Trent wouldn't do for his brother. Occasionally when they were dining like this Vivienne would glance at him, dressed for the casino, all ready to go and pick up the gamblers' money, and she would wonder how it was possible for a man to have two such opposing sides to his character. Because of her thoughts she never had much to say to him. He in turn, when he wasn't regarding her with that veiled scepticism, kept her at a cool distance. But they tried to give the impression of being smilingly in tune for Robert's sake. He was the guest of honour, sitting in his wheelchair at the head of the table, and everything was done to keep the atmosphere lighthearted, but somehow their jokes didn't quite come off.

Robert was extremely sensitive to these things and Vivienne worried that he would notice the discord between her and Trent, yet she couldn't help herself. More often than not her remarks to Trent would carry a touch of acid. One evening after dinner beside the window, Robert had been settled back against the pillows in bed and Trent was getting ready to leave for the casino. 'Don't sit up too late, old son.' He gave his brother that special smile. 'Lots of rest and you'll be down at that pool again in no time.'

'I'll watch it, Trent,' Robert said earnestly. 'Just a couple of card games with Viv, then I'll definitely hit the sack.'

'Goodnight, Vivienne,' Trent nodded her way as she set up the card table, and turning at the door he tacked on laconically, 'Watch out for the chemin de fer and poker. I'd make it gin rummy if I were you.'

'We play for fun, not for money,' she retorted smoothly, and her carping smile was aimed his way as he went out. 'Unlike your customers, we've nothing to lose.'

The door closed and there was silence for a while. Then Robert said with a wan kind of humour from the pillows, 'You don't like Trent, do you, Viv?'

'It isn't a question of liking or disliking,' she tried to inject lightness into her tones. 'He's your brother. I go along with that.'

'I know what it is that rattles you. But you're wrong about him, you know.' Robert looked at her whimsically.

Seeing that he was determined to pursue the matter, Vivienne said good-naturedly, 'All right, you tell me what it is that rattles me.'

'No, I think it's a fair question—me asking you,' he countered with a grin.

'Very well.' She took a breath. Her voice quivered slightly with feeling, though she had wanted to sound off-hand. 'Let's say I don't like the way he earns his money.'

'That's straight from the shoulder anyway.' Robert's grin

was crooked. He patted the bed beside him. 'Come and sit here by me.'

She put the cards down and did as he asked, and when she was settled he spoke meditatively from the pillows. 'I was two when our parents were slaughtered in a native up-rising in what was then the Belgian Congo. Trent was six-teen. There was just about enough money for him to finish his schooling. After that he took charge of me. I don't re-member much about those early years except that he was always there when I needed him. Later when I was in my teens he encouraged me to do what I wanted with my life.' Robert smiled absently. 'He wasn't too excited about rugby, thought it was a dead-end kind of profession. But once he knew it was in my blood he went all out to get me launched, and travelled when he couldn't really spare the time, to see me play in important matches. Then this muscular bug hit me. You'd have thought Trent would have told me it was my own fault—all those heavy falls and rough tackles—but he didn't. He took me to every doctor who knew about my disease in the hope of finding a cure. Pretty lost cause, but you couldn't tell Trent that.'

Vivienne squeezed his hand. Not for anything would she give any sign of the lump in her throat.

'Then he heard of these two French doctors in Tangier,' Robert went on, 'who were specialising in this thing I've got, which has an unpronounceable name. Before you knew it Trent was over here looking for a house where we could stay. He bought Koudia as it stands, hired staff and got these rooms fixed up for me. What it costs him for my weekly trips to the hospital and the doctors' services is any-body's guess.'

Vivienne was still holding his hand. Despite his illness he looked strikingly big and muscular set back among the pil-lows. His young handsome face was flushed with talk. She spoke feelingly. 'It's right that you should have all these things, Robert. You deserve the best—I know that. Just because it bothers me that all this,' she waved an arm around the opulent furnishings—'comes from the gamblers pockets it doesn't mean——'

Robert shook his head and gave her a kind of pitying gleam. 'That's what I've been meaning to tell you. I guess I'm going the long way round about it.' It was his turn to give her hand a squeeze as he went on, 'Trent's been a lot of things in his life ... explorer, interpreter, prospector, soldier.' He saw Vivienne's look and grinned. 'That surprises you, huh? Well, you have to remember that our parents were a little colourful that way. Dad was a trade development organiser for north and central Africa, and in the end that's what Trent inherited, I suppose, his business sense. He saw the boom potential in the expanding cities, and ore and mineral development, and went ahead with his ideas. Now he's rich. Through oil mainly, and copper.'

'Oil?' Vivienne looked blank. 'But the casino ...?'

'Let me finish,' Robert said gently. 'We were in England, remember. Trent had sold all his business interests to devote his time to me. But you know,' a low chuckle, 'it was a bit like taking an old lady's knitting away from her. He was lost. When we came to Tangier he looked around for something to do, but it had to be a business that would allow him plenty of free time. That's why he bought the casino—so that he could work nights while I was in bed, and have the days free to spend with me. So you see,' Robert concluded, 'he hasn't always been a casino mogul. That's what you thought, isn't it?'

'Yes ... yes, it is,' Vivienne replied in a fog, and as she made to mouth a question Robert laughed.

'Oh, sure, he makes money. But that's Trent.' Talk had used up the time and he added drowsily, 'Let's skip the cards Viv. I'm ready for some shut-eye. And if I can show Trent that I'm okay in the wheelchair he'll let me come down to the pool again.'

She kissed him lightly and smoothed his covers as he settled down. On the way out she tapped on the door of Haroun's room as a signal that she was leaving. She made her way to her own quarters still in a mist at what Robert had told her. And yet in a way didn't it all add up? This house, with its ornate French furnishings and exquisite antique clutter—she had always felt that it didn't somehow have Trent's stamp of personality on it.

It was rather odd now dining with Trent in the evenings. Vivienne found herself resenting what Robert had told her. She felt a kind of nakedness without her armour of distaste, and at moments she was inclined to flounder inwardly when she looked across the table at him, groomed and courteous, perhaps offering her more wine, or chatting to Momeen about the quality of the food.

Another factor perhaps, to do with her vulnerability, was the strain of the past few days. Robert's collapse had shocked her badly. He was so young, and one didn't—couldn't associate incurability with the husky handsome figure that he was. She had wanted to do all she could to get him back to his mobile self, and she had succeeded; at considerable cost to herself. She had become a little thinner. Her features were finely drawn and curiously enhanced by the lilac shadows under her eyes and loosely waving hair with its auburn lights.

Trent's gaze rested on her often. They seldom dined with Robert now because he was back to expending his energies at the pool and life around the house had returned to normal. One evening when she had eaten little at the dinner table the senior brother said, 'You need a change. Rob's sleeping better at nights, so he doesn't need you twenty-four hours a day. Why don't you take a break?'

They had drifted to their usual spot at the window with its view of the shadowy-lit Casbah and beaded lights of the city. Vivienne was wearing a white sleeveless blouse with a crisp upstanding collar, and a neat black skirt. A tiny pearl in each ear was the only decoration she had allowed herself. After she had inhaled on the cigarette under which he held the flame of his lighter she enquired flippantly, 'Where would you suggest? A run out to the Bubana country club, or a night at the bull ring?'

Trent shrugged humorously. 'You only have to say the word. You've got the car at your disposal. By the way,' his eyes narrowed as he pulled on his cigarette, 'Abdul tells me you haven't requested his services for some time.'

'There's been nothing to see,' she said quickly. And then casually, 'Even Tangier has its limits to a sightseer.'

'And you're no sightseer, we both know that,' he replied lazily.

The trend of the conversation had the quality of quicksand. In an endeavour to return to solid ground she said lightly, 'But as you've pointed out, even I need some diversion at times. The trouble is, in the more sophisticated types of entertainment Abdul would stand out like a sore finger——'

'And there's no question of you going alone,' he finished for her. He took a thoughtful tug on his cigarette and while he studied the view Vivienne traced his profile with her gaze. She had come to know that jawline well; the nose, lacking the straight youthful lines of Robert's, yet it was a nose that gave strength to the rest of his features. She knew the way he flexed his shoulders, expensively clad now in the white dinner jacket, to illustrate a point; the odd habit he had of flicking his cigarette with an upward tap; how his smile could have a razor-edged coolness if he felt that way. He had, she decided, a kind of hard-bitten polish; a manner which commanded respect.

He turned suddenly, upsetting her musings, and said, 'I know somewhere where you would be free to wander alone and not be bothered by anyone.'

'In Tangier?' She tilted a disbelieving eyebrow.

'That's right.' His grin was slightly ironic. 'Why not drop in at the Café Anglais? You can have a drink and wander among the roulette tables and feel perfectly safe.'

'The casino!' She sounded shocked.

'Where the witch herself holds her high court in the hall of the green tables,' he drawled with a challenging gleam.

The idea shook her a little. But was it such a bad one? Trent ran the casino as a pastime, she knew that now. And

she needed a break from Koudia. She toyed with the notion.
'Well ... It would be an experience ...'

'Get Abdul to drive you down about ten-thirty,' said
Trent, stubbing out his cigarette. 'Business should be in full
swing by then.'

As he turned to go Vivienne asked a little breathlessly,
'How do I dress?'

'You're okay as you are.' His glance swept over her.
'Bring a wrap. It might be late by the time you're ready to
leave.'

She turned back to the window as he went out, her heart
beating erratically. She never thought she would be joining
Trent in an atmosphere she had once despised.

She had an hour and a half to kill. The time dragged. Up
in her room she applied a fresh touch of make-up and
brushed her hair. She changed her shoes for a pair of black
evening sandals and found a black velvet purse that
matched, and a lacy wrap. At last it was time to go downstairs and Abdul was waiting as she had requested in the
limousine out on the drive.

It didn't take them long to reach the city with its cosmo-
politan crowds, and from there the narrow alley near the
sea where Vivienne was reminded of her scuffle with the
Moroccan youths and Trent's appearance. Abdul parked
the car and led the way through the gloom. The Café
Anglais was a sea-front establishment and one saw nothing
of its gaily-lit frontage until one turned the corner of the
alley and met the bracing air of the Atlantic.

Abdul escorted her inside, sweeping past the nods and
bows of deference from the native staff, with true Arab
disdain. Vivienne looked around her. She saw Robert's
description of the casino was fairly accurate. The café area
was white stucco walls with elaborately styled Moorish
archways showing views of the tables section where people
chatted desultorily in an atmosphere wholly Moroccan.
There *were* parrots on the wall in heavy wrought iron cages
like lanterns, and low-slung lampshades, and ornately
carved bar-type swing doors. Some of the men, Europeans,

were playing chess. Turbaned and uniformed attendants moved back and forth.

From a distant archway Trent came to meet them. 'So you made it.' Vivienne felt unaccountably shy standing there beside Abdul. Trent was his usual suave self. 'Don't be nervous,' he joked, putting a hand on her elbow. 'I promise I won't surrender you to the clutches of the riotous daughters of hell.' And guiding her forward, 'Come on, I'll show you around.'

Abdul left them and Trent escorted her to the far archway. Through here was a kind of mosaic-tiled interior with potted palms, and across more archways from which came the low buzz of conversation and the drift of cigarette smoke. Walking with him, offering a shy smile as he nodded to members of the staff posted at intervals beside the archways, Vivienne recalled that Trent had always been idly laconic with her and not a little amused at what she had considered his vices in running the casino. It irritated her to know that he had never felt it necessary to justify his actions to her.

He led her across the mosaic-tiled space to the second line of archways and into an interior which had something of a low-key party atmosphere. Around the green baize tables was a motley collection of people—men in smart evening dress, Moroccan army officers wearing dashing turbanned headdress, young men and girls in hippy-type clothing, dazzling-gowned females, velvet-clad dowagers and tall Arabs in Western dress and brick-red tarboushes. Some sat at the tables, placing stakes and reacting to the calls of the croupiers with no noticeable change of expression. Others were mainly onlookers and gave tiny squeaks or groans according to how the numbers went.

'Not exactly Monte Carlo,' Trent quipped as he guided Vivienne around pointing out the various games in progress. 'But it's enough to keep those who like to flirt occasionally with Lady Luck amused.' As she watched the croupiers with their wooden shovels and listened to the clicking of the ball that spun for roulette he told her, 'Later

I'll arrange for you to be given a few chips and you can try your hand against the wheel or the cards, but right now it's time we had that drink.' He led her out through an archway and along the palm-lined vestibule to a door at the far end.

Trent's office was a long windowless room with black quilted walls decorated with gold studs and a huge desk to match. There were gold-threaded divans and the opposite wall was given over entirely to a glittering glassed-in bar. The decor was totally different from the rest of the casino and Vivienne guessed it was a legacy of the previous owner.

Trent went to one of the glass-fronted shelves and brought a bottle and two glasses to the desk. He poured liberally and handing Vivienne her glass and leaning against the desk with his own asked with lazy humour, 'How does it feel to be actually here in the Palace of Sin?'

'You can tease if you like,' she sipped at her drink and twinkled primly, 'but I happen to think that gambling is a malaise.'

'Like housewives losing all the housekeeping money at the local bingo?' he said with a mocking gleam.

'On a lesser scale, yes,' she agreed lightly. Then nodding darkly in the direction of the gaming rooms, 'I've a feeling that some of those out there have a lot more to worry about than the few pounds it takes to run a home for a week.'

'You're thinking of the old days when fortunes were made and lost overnight,' Trent said easily. 'It's not like that now. Money's a lot more evenly spent, for one thing. And those who have it generally know how to stick to it.'

She twirled her glass in her hand and slanted him a quizzical look. 'Are you telling me that no one these days—to use a gambling term, I think—loses his shirt?'

'Of course, there are the compulsive gamblers,' he admitted from his lounging position. 'The ones who derive a kind of morbid satisfaction from losing. But if they didn't come to the Café Anglais they'd find some other place to go and take a knock at chance because it's in their blood, this urge to compete with life.'

Vivienne looked at him with a frustrated gleam. 'Men always have this knack of turning an argument to their own advantage.'

'Naturally,' he sloped a grin. 'We train at it from birth.'

A light tap on the door interrupted the chat. A stocky, elderly man wearing the royal blue evening dress of the casino staff came in. Trent said, 'André, my chief croupier.'

'Madame.' André clicked his heels at Vivienne, then turned to say something in low tones to his chief. Trent nodded, walked to the bar and to Vivienne's inward surprise opened back a shelved compartment of bottles to reveal a very sturdy-looking safe. He opened the vault and counted out several thick wads of Moroccan currency. When the croupier had departed with the money he said in a dry voice, 'That was for someone who broke the bank. So you see, the casino doesn't win all the time.' He looked at his watch and finished his drink. 'Time I was circulating among the clientele.' He wrote out a chit for her at the desk while she was finding somewhere to leave her glass and guiding her to the door he told her, 'Take this to the cashier's window and ask for whatever you want. When you've had enough give me the word and I'll get Abdul to drive you home.'

He went with her back to the gaming rooms where he was immediately claimed by a red-faced colonel type who beamed at his appearance and thrust out a hand as though he were a long-lost friend. The place was crowded now and Vivienne wandered a little aimlessly around the tables. She didn't bother to cash the chit that Trent had given her. She didn't know what she wanted out of the evening, but one thing she was certain of: it wasn't money.

She did make an effort to take an interest in what was going on, watching the inscrutable faces of the people at the tables and the way they played the numbers. Abdul, looking very much a part of the scene among the other fez-wearing Arabs, circulated unobtrusively among the patrons, his duties no doubt to keep a sharp eye open for dishonest play and trouble-makers. Vivienne smiled to herself, thinking that with his Moorish hauteur and implacable air he was ideally suited to the job.

For the best part of an hour she strolled around, telling herself that at least it was a change from pacing her room at Koudia. It was when she was on the point of searching out Trent to say that she was ready to leave that something happened which drained the life from her where she stood.

Being concerned with the only kind of gambling she understood, the roulette wheels, she had paid little attention to the big chemin-de-fer table in the centre of the room. The players grouped around it came into her glance for the first time as she scanned the room for Trent, and it was then that her heart stood still. That thin figure in the worn looking suit gazing intensely at the cards in his hands. Wasn't there something familiar in the way his hair receded from that high forehead ... in the nervous jut of his chin ...? The blood rushed to her head, almost blinding her. Long before her consciousness could come to grips with the miracle, her heart was joyfully pealing out the news to her. Gary! Gary! It was Gary!

Hastily she looked around her, thinking that everyone must know of her feverish happiness, but she soon saw that the atmosphere in the room was unchanged. It was only inside herself where brilliant rainbows shone. There was a brightness in her eyes as she made her way over to the central table. It was odd, strangely nerve-tingling to be so near to Gary now that she could touch his sleeve. She hoped that he would look up so that she could laugh at his surprise. He was listening to the crooning tones of the croupier, 'Faites vos jeux, messieurs et dames,' his eyes riveted on his cards. He remained in this position for so long that in the end she was driven to tugging his sleeve and saying shyly, 'Hello, Gary. It's been a long time.'

He looked at her with unseeing eyes which came to life fleetingly as he tried to place her. Then he said in between keeping a watch on his cards, 'It's Viv, isn't it?'

'I'm flattered,' she laughed over the let-down feeling inside her. 'You still remember my name!'

She saw that he wasn't listening. He uttered some gambling term, '*Banco seul*,' then swore beneath his breath. 'Damn!' The croupier was crooning in French again. Vivienne moved closer to Gary. His whole attention was trained on the table, so she said with a twinkle,

'Would it surprise you to know that I've been searching for you all over Tangier?'

Something went wrong again. He swore, and with exasperation in his tones he shot her a look. 'Not now! Can't you see I'm busy?'

Vivienne had no time to react much to this comment because at a distance she saw Trent and it was clear that he was looking for her. She knew that he had spotted her. He was making his way over. She said, hoping to catch Gary's attention with her smile and her hopeful look, 'I have to go now. Perhaps ...?' His mind was on the game and she dared not stay. Swiftly she moved off, going forward to meet Trent.

'I've been looking for you,' he eyed her searchingly and smiled. 'One or two of the new arrivals have had a little too much to drink, and I'd feel easier if you were out of it. Abdul's waiting.'

Vivienne went out with him mechanically. She remembered little of their walk through to the café area where he handed her over to Abdul, or the car journey home. The only thing that kept pounding, pounding ecstatically in her brain was that she had seen Gary; found him after the weeks of fruitless search. Back in her room at Koudia she whirled, hugging the knowledge to her. Just think! She had looked everywhere and he must have been there at the casino, not exactly under her nose, but closely connected as the Café Anglais was with her life here at Koudia, one could almost have said so. Oh, life was ironic indeed!

She hardly slept that night, and the following day it was difficult to appear her usual composed self with this inner rapture giving her the feeling of walking on air. Towards late afternoon, after a lazy game of croquet and a session at the pool with Robert, she began to wonder how she could contrive another visit to the casino. It was a sobering thought, this feeling she had that Gary spent most of his time there. She felt practically certain that whatever night she might happen to visit there again she would find him at one of the gambling tables. Drying off her hair in the sun, she cast a quick glance at Trent, chatting smilingly with his brother over a drink. It was going to be awkward working something out without arousing his suspicions.

That evening at dinner she decided that the easiest way was to play it naturally. After the final course, when they were lingering over a rather fine claret, she said casually, 'Are you expecting a full house at the casino tonight?'

Trent leaned back in his chair and replied with a smile, 'The Café Anglais never actually bulges at the seams. We've got the regulars, of course, and with the summer approaching there's always the tourists, but it's the kind of entertainment that attracts only a steady influx of customers. I prefer it that way.' He reached for his glass, then referred, as she had hoped he would, to her visit last night. 'Do I take it that your tour of the gaming rooms left a lingering interest?'

She looked past his mocking gleam and replied lightly, 'You could say that. I found it fascinating watching the various types at the tables, though I'd never want to go through their kind of agony waiting for the right numbers.'

'I know,' said Trent with a dry grin. 'I was told you didn't exchange the chit I gave you.' He added as an afterthought, 'If you enjoyed the trip you must do it again some time.'

'Oh, could I? I mean ...' Hastily she lowered her eager gaze and searched for some valid excuse. 'I thought, as Robert's sleeping, there's no real sense in my hanging about the house. I have been rather tied to it lately, and ... well, it's just nice to have a change of scene.'

'I couldn't agree more,' said Trent, watching her. 'Besides, I need Abdul at the casino, so that way we both get what we want.' He finished his drink and rose, and coming round to ease her chair away as she got up he told her in his suave way, 'Feel free to drop in at the Café Anglais any time. I'll do my best to make your evenings as pleasant as possible.'

'Oh no, please!' Her glance flew to his where he stood behind her chair. 'Don't make any special effort for me. I'll be quite content just to drift around on my own.'

'You might have to some of the time,' he said easily. 'But I shall want it known that you're to have whatever you wish while you're under my roof. What kind of a casino owner would I be if I couldn't do that for my brother's girl?' He was standing close to her where she had risen from her chair. His gaze lingered on her over-long, she thought. She battled with an uncomfortable feeling. Then he said in clipped tones, 'Goodnight, Vivienne. I take it I'll be seeing you later on.'

She nodded, containing the breathless excitement in her until she had heard him leave in his car. Upstairs in her room she hunted for something to wear that would remind Gary of their summer together. It was unfortunate that she possessed nothing of the rather juvenile wardrobe of those days and it occurred to her that it might be foolish to try and go back to the jeans and leather-thonged shirts image of the past. That was four years ago, a dead episode. She was a woman now and her approach, quite naturally, would be different.

After some thought she put on a white dress and added a little gold jacket to give an evening effect. She had gold shoes and an evening bag to match, and dabbing herself liberally with perfume before the mirror she thought the finished result wasn't bad. Her hair had a healthy shine and the anticipatory sparkle in her eyes dispelled the fatigue of the last few days.

When she considered she had killed enough time she went downstairs and told Abdul to bring the car. Her heart was knocking badly as they drove down towards the sea. What if Gary wasn't there after all? What if she had been wrong in deducing that he spent most evenings at the casino? She felt she would never live through the disappointment if this were so.

Abdul led the way into the Café Anglais and foolishly Vivienne's eyes scanned the people at the tables. It was early yet by casino standards, but still her glance hopefully searched the corners. Abdul left her, giving her his polite salaam, and she relaxed a little. Now she was free to wander as she pleased. The place was fairly crowded. Her heart started up its tattoo again. It was not impossible that Gary was here somewhere, taking the first drink of the evening before going through to the gaming rooms.

The café area was made up of several archwayed sections. She was passing through one of these when she almost collided with Trent. If she hadn't been searching the place with her gaze she would have seen him. As it was, it was too late to do anything but laugh at her folly.

'Well, well.' He steadied her with both hands then let his gaze roam over her. 'Very pretty—the get-up. And you smell like a flower garden.' One hand lingered on her arm. 'I'm just on my way to the office. I think we've got time to open a bottle of something before the casino starts filling up.'

'I'm honoured,' she replied flippantly, allowing him to propel her forward. What else could she do? She dared not give him so much as a hint as to what was really going on in her mind.

In the black and gold office he went to the bar and brought an expensive vintage and crystal glasses to the desk. But they had barely sampled the golden liquid when Marcel came in. He apologised for the interruption and while he ironed out some difficulty with Trent, Vivienne made a leisurely tour of the office, glass in hand.

The chief croupier departed. A few minutes later Trent was showing her the desk ashtray shaped in the form of a roulette wheel when the door opened again and one of the turbanned bar attendants came in with a list in his hand which seemed to cause him some puzzlement. Trent was doing some explaining when Vivienne interrupted to say softly, 'You're obviously busy. I'll go and amuse myself somewhere. Please carry on.'

He left the bar attendant and the list for a moment and escorted her to the door. As he opened it for her he said with a harassed grin, 'I've made it clear to the staff that you're to have the run of the place, but if you're in doubt about anything ask Abdul. I'll see you in the gaming rooms a little later on.'

Vivienne digested this last remark as she moved off. All she could hope was that Trent would be kept busy in his office long enough for her to make some contact with Gary. She went straight to the gaming rooms, but although they were filling up there was no one as yet by the chemin-de-fer table and no sign of Gary in any other part of the salon. She thought it might be useful to take another trip to the café area. Wandering casually through the archways, casting an oblique glance around the tables, she noticed the imperceptible bows from the uniformed staff. They had seen her with Trent and were conforming to his wishes that she be treated with the utmost courtesy. She smiled in reply from time to time, although it was a little unnerving to know that she had complete freedom in so sophisticated an establishment.

She mused around at the bar with its typically Moorish decor for a while, then retraced her steps back to the gaming salon. This time her heart did its familiar somersault when she entered. She spotted Gary almost at once over by the far roulette table. Fortunately he appeared to be watching play rather than participating, not like last night when his mind had been wholly occupied with the cards in his hand. Swiftly Vivienne made her way over. The players were fairly sparsely spread around the table and she was able to slide in comfortably alongside Gary. She spoke up facetiously but firmly to attract his attention away from the musical rhythm of the roulette ball. 'Hello again. Still trying for the big stakes?'

Gary took the joke a little sourly, she thought. He turned

his head slightly, ran his glance over her and said absently, 'So it *was* you I saw here last night. I wasn't sure whether I'd dreamt it.'

'Did it seem like a dream?' she asked, with a breathless smile, and softly with the suggestion of stars in her eyes. 'It's been all of four years, Gary.'

'Your name kept going round and round in my mind,' he said as though he hadn't heard her. 'Then I had it! Vivienne Blyth from the Hotel Riadh days.' He thrust a hand into his jacket pocket and asked while he fumbled there, 'How have you been?'

'Oh ...' Vivienne was all set to make some lighthearted reply when he drew out some gambling chips and muttered, 'Excuse me a second.' He studied his meagre pile of chips, carefully placed half of them on various numbers on the table, then as the croupier's voice came over to warn that the wheel was about to spin he split his attention between her and the table again. 'You were saying?'

'Oh, nothing!' she replied lightly, and commenting mischievously on his choice of numbers she asked, 'Why didn't you put them all on the one that brings you luck? Your birthday or something. Think what you'd win if it came up.'

'You never rely on luck in this game.' He waited for the wheel to stop. 'One has to calculate.'

The ball came to rest and his chips went down. To take his mind off his disappointment she asked cheerfully, 'How has life been treating you?'

'Can't grumble,' he shrugged, weighing up the last of his chips. 'I'm in photography now. Dropped the music game. Too many kids at it.'

The croupier's voice cut in again. There was the excited chatter of the other players around them. Vivienne said, in the hope of drawing him away, 'It's not the ideal place for a conversation. Why don't we ...?'

'Just a minute.' Gary fingered his chips and studied the table. He said to her with a flicker of impatience, 'One should follow the game really.'

He didn't bet that time and Vivienne spoke up again. 'I

was saying, why don't we go for a drink? We could talk about old times ...'

'We'll do that some time,' he nodded, his eyes on the table. He was doing some kind of mental arithmetic and Vivienne threw a quick glance round the room. She had told herself she would keep a wary eye open for Trent, now there he was over by the far archway. Her heart began to pound nervously as she looked his way. Had he spotted her chatting away to Gary before she had noticed him?

CHAPTER SIX

SHE met Trent towards the centre of the gaming room. He said, taking her arm, 'The place is filling up and we've got the usual society types who enjoy being seen at the notorious Café Anglais. Come on over and meet a few.'

Vivienne relaxed at the thread of amusement in his tones. Over the disappointment in her at Gary's tepid reception she put on a smile for the ordeal to come.

'Trent, my dear boy! I was just saying to Cynthia here ... hello, hello, hello!' The man with the air force officer moustache eyed Vivienne up and down with a devilish gleam as she approached on Trent's arm. He introduced her lazily as his brother's girl-friend and she met the curious smiles and stares of the group lounging near the gaming room bar; society types indeed, judging by the svelte, expensive gowns of the females, and tailored perfection of the men's evening dress.

'I was telling Cynthia,' the man with the moustache spoke over the babble of the others. 'You ought to install a first-class French restaurant, my dear fellow, like we have at Cannes. You'd do a bomb with the casino crowd.'

'This is Morocco, Derek,' Trent said agreeably. 'The Café Anglais made its reputation on local dishes served in typical surroundings.'

'In that case, darling, oughtn't it to be called Café Marocain or something,' someone drawled teasingly.

'I agree with Trent.' Another voice spoke up. 'You can get French food in the Eiffel hotel. We want *cous-cous* and *pastella*.'

'But not before baccarat, darling.' A mature woman in oyster satin cast an eager glance to where play was in progress. 'I knew a man who won a fortune, you know. Doubled his stake thirty times and ...'

'And lost the lot the next evening, I bet.' There was uproarious laughter. A kittenish female pouted, 'If I lost Trent would accept my diamond bracelet as surety, wouldn't you, darling?'

'No trinkets allowed on the gaming tables,' Trent quipped. 'Rules of the house.' He ordered a drink for Vivienne and she found herself enjoying the sophisticated wit of the group. With Trent draping an arm idly across her shoulders it was easy to join in the conversation and the time passed without her realising it. She had no thought of leaving until the party drifted towards the gaming tables and Trent told her, 'It's getting late. Time Abdul was taking you home. I sent him into the café earlier to deal with a slight rumpus there. I'll go and see if he's smoothed things over.'

Vivienne nodded absently, lingering near the bar. She was surprised to see when she looked at her watch that it was almost one o'clock. She was half-listening to two turtanned Moors nearby talking in rapid Spanish when a hand touched her wrist and she turned to find Gary standing beside her. 'Hello, again,' he said, smiling broadly. 'Can I buy you a drink?'

'No, thank you. I've just had one,' Vivienne replied a little breathlessly. She looked at him and asked, 'Did you have a good win?'

'No. Lost the lot,' Gary shrugged. 'But I'm learning to be a good loser.' He seemed thoughtful and as though wanting to appear offhand he added with a grin, 'I saw you with Trent Colby, the big boss himself. Is he a friend of yours?'

'I suppose you could say that in a way,' Vivienne replied.

'How come you know him so well?' Gary offered her a cigarette. She declined and said with a smile and a sigh, 'It's a long story.'

'I like listening to stories,' he quirked. 'And anyway, weren't we going to talk over old times together?'

Vivienne's gaze was on the archways. Panic in her eyes, she said suddenly, breaking away from him, 'I'm sorry, Gary, I have to go. Trent's on his way over.'

Gary appeared to size up the situation swiftly. He said with a pained grin, 'Well, if you can't talk now, how about metting me tomorrow at the Scheherezade ... at three o'clock?'

Vivienne's mind worked rapidly. Tomorrow was Robert's day for the hospital. Trent usually kept to himself in the house. Could she? Dared she? She said quickly over her singing heart, 'All right,' and moved away.

Trent arrived before she had got more than a few steps away from the bar. He took her arm and said, guiding her out, 'The café's still a bit rowdy—a bunch from one of the cruise ships living it up a bit. I'll take you through myself.'

At the outside door Abdul was waiting. Vivienne said goodnight to Trent, hoping there were no tell-tale stars in her eyes, and went out to the car with the Arab manservant. Her mood alternated between glowing happiness and panic and worry on the ride back to Koudia. What had she done, saying she would meet Gary in town in broad daylight? What if someone saw them? Still there was no slackening of her pulses despite the danger. She would go, of course. How could she help herself?

The following day she kept mainly to her room, finding little chores to do so that she wouldn't run into Trent. She couldn't avoid lunching with him, but as the day was hot he had ordered the meal to be served out of doors, and with Momeen tripping back and forth and Abdul hovering over the food trolley the strain wasn't so great.

Around half past two when the house was still and silent she walked casually down the stairs, her heart hammering in case she ran into Trent. It wouldn't have mattered, because she often went for a stroll round the grounds at this time of day. But there was something about what she was planning which filled her with distaste when she thought of Trent. Better for her conscience that he was nowhere about.

She took the route to the domed summerhouse where she sometimes sat with Robert gazing out to sea, and from here it was an easy matter to pick her way down the shallow slope into the fruit orchards. There were paths everywhere and Berber women working, so there seemed little chance of her being spotted from the house. Just the same she felt easier when at last she reached the main gates which opened almost on to city streets. Five minutes on foot and she was able to hail a taxi. She arrived at the Scheherezade a little before three.

The café, next to the Grand Mosque, was one favoured by tourists. They could sip their drinks to the accompaniment of Arab music and browse among the displays of Moorish embroidery and leatherwork. Vivienne looked round eagerly, fearing that she would never find Gary among the crowds, but yes, there he was at one of the alcove tables inside. It struck her fleetingly that he was practising discretion through no prompting from her.

He rose to meet her and she hurried in to him, her lips parted in a palpitating smile. She thought he might have commented on the pretty sun-dress she was wearing, but he simply indicated the seat opposite him and asked, 'What shall I order?'

Nestled in the alcove seat across from him, she said with a nostalgic gleam, 'Why don't we have a Cinzano?'

'In this heat?' He pulled a face. 'I'll have a cold beer.'

Vivienne settled for iced lime. Philosophically she told herself that, four years older, she had no taste for Cinzano either. The drinks arrived and Gary held up his glass in a brief toast before swallowing thirstily. He was wearing a white open-necked shirt and dark trousers and from the moment she entered Vivienne had been mildly shocked at his appearance. His hair was coarse and thinning and there were lines around his eyes and mouth that she hadn't noticed in the casino. But he was still the same old Gary, the man who could set her pulses racing four years ago and who was doing just that right now.

She gazed at him and said softly, 'Tell me about yourself. I'm longing to know what's been happening to you while I've been in England.'

'Not much.' He gave the familiar shrug. 'I told you my

life story last night. I'm in the photography business with a Jibaldi. He stands on the Rue de Fez and snaps the passers-by and I do the developing. Nothing earth-shaking, but it's a living.'

'And the casino?' she asked with a twinkle.

'It's the only place where one has a chance to make a packet. It can be done, I've seen it happen. I don't intend to spend my life pegging up negatives for a Jibaldi.' He finished his beer and placing the glass down said, bringing his gaze up to hers, 'Talking of the casino, last night you were going to tell me how you come to know Colby, the owner, so well.' He added with a grin as though wanting to make light of his remark, 'It's not every day that one meets a close associate of one of the richest men in Tangier.'

'As I told you, it's a long story,' Vivienne smiled.

'We've got all afternoon.' He reached for cigarettes.

She waited until he was leaning back with one, then said with a half laugh, 'You're not going to believe it.'

'Try me.' He drew on his cigarette. She thought she detected a flicker of impatience in the gesture.

'Well, it's all to do with Lucy, my friend.' Of course she wouldn't have divulged the secret to a soul, but Gary was someone special and soon she found herself pouring out the whole story to him. She told him all about the pen-pal relationship that had blossomed into a romance and how Lucy had sent her photograph and then found out that Robert was so ill she couldn't bear to tell him the truth. How she, Vivienne, had agreed to pretend that she was really the writer of the letters, and how she had been living at Koudia playing the part of Lucy these past weeks.

'I see,' Gary's eyes narrowed through the cigarette smoke. 'You mean the kid has no idea that you two girls have done a swap?'

'None,' Vivienne replied. 'Trent sent for Lucy when he knew there was no hope and I arrived in her place. Robert's very happy, and that's the most important thing. This way he need never know.'

'Yes, I see what you mean.' Gary ran his fingers round

the rim of his beer glass and asked, 'Is the kid really incurably ill?'

'I'm afraid so,' Vivienne sighed. 'He's much weaker now than when I first came and he always comes back from his day at the hospital exhausted.' She was suddenly bitter and her amber eyes were liquid with affection. 'How can life be so cruel? If anyone deserved to live it's Robert. He's a fine young man, gentle-natured and unselfish, I'm very fond of him. I'd never do anything to hurt him.' She finished her musings and came to with an apologetic smile. 'So you see how it is, why I had to rush away from you last night. If Trent ever got to know the truth . . .' She shuddered at the thought.

Gary said, 'I take it Colby thinks a lot of his kid brother?'

Vivienne spoke with wry humour. 'That's an understatement, if ever I heard one. He worships Robert. He spends all his time sheltering him from hurt of any kind.' She shrugged. 'We all do. Robert's that sort of person. You feel you want to do everything to protect him.'

Gary, still fingering his glass, commented, his tight grin back again, 'But it can't be that bad living up there in the lush villa that everybody can see from Tangier? They say it's filled with French art treasures.'

'I haven't noticed,' Vivienne said simply. 'I spend most of my time outdoors. Robert can still swim and there's nothing he likes more than . . .'

She saw that Gary wasn't listening. He was stubbing out his cigarette and seemed lost in thought. Then glancing at his watch he said, 'It's time I was going.'

'So soon!' Vivienne couldn't hide her disappointment. 'I thought you said you had all afternoon?'

'I was being generous with myself. Actually I ought to be getting back to the photo-lab.' His smile did nothing to ease her disappointment, not until he took hold of her hand and said with some of his old urgency, 'I've got to see you again. What about tonight at the casino?'

Vivienne knew an overwhelming joy, but she drew on her lip worriedly. 'It's risky, Gary.' And thinking he hadn't quite understood the situation she explained, 'Don't forget Trent believes that I'm in love with his brother. It wouldn't look right if I appeared friendly with other men at the casino.'

'I don't see what he would find odd about it,' Gary shrugged. 'Engaged girls, even married ones, enjoy the company of other men occasionally when they're out for the evening. What more natural than chatting to a mere acquaintance from time to time?'

He was right, of course, Vivienne pondered. Hadn't she done just that last night? The inimitable Derek with the handlebar moustache had flirted with her outrageously and Trent hadn't thought anything about that. She nodded before she could change her mind. 'All right. But not tonight. I usually spend some time with Robert when he's been away from the house all day. Tomorrow night.' She knew she was asking a lot, but Gary didn't seem to mind the clandestine meetings.

'Fair enough. If we wait until the casino fills up a bit, around eleven, no one will notice us. Must dash.' He rose and left her and she realised that he hadn't paid for the drinks. But that was a minor detail. Her cheeks were flushed with happiness as she searched for the correct coins in her bag. She saw nothing of the sun-starved tourists basking in the brilliance of the afternoon as she went out, or the teeming street with its loaded donkeys and noisy pedlars. While she was waving a taxi down it occurred to her also that they hadn't got around to talking about old times after all. Still, she climbed into her seat feeling blissfully content. There would be plenty of opportunity for that now. Gary had asked to see her again. And he understood about Robert. What more could one ask for?

That evening she set herself out to be particularly attentive towards Robert. He arrived back from the hospital grey-faced and asking only for his bed. She went up in the lift with him and got out his pyjamas and bed robe. Trent who had come up with them didn't suggest that they all dine together in his room. He knew that his brother was

too tired. Vivienne had changed into an apple-green dress
and brushed her hair so that it fell in loose dark waves. She
singled out books of poetry for the bedside table, and filled
the crystal carafe with fresh water. She felt Trent's eyes on
her as she moved about the room and wished she didn't
have this guilty feeling. After all, she told herself, she was
playing her part in the tragedy to the best of her ability, and
in the meantime she had her own life to lead. Yet she felt
wretched just knowing that Robert was suffering.

Trent went downstairs to change before dinner. Vivienne
planned to sit with Robert for a while. Settled back among
the pillows now, he glanced at the dozens of small bottles
beside him and joked hollowly, 'All these pills and not one
of them contains that new lease of life.'

Vivienne was sat on the bed beside him. She would have
given anything to take away the look of hopelessness and
dread in his eyes. He pulled her to him and buried his face
in her shoulder. 'Hold me, Viv. Hold me close.'

She and Trent ate dinner in silence that evening. There
was an air about the house that sickness brings. Even the
effusive Momeen was subdued as he served the meal.
Vivienne went to her room once Trent left for the casino.
Haroun was back from his day in town and would be on
hand if Robert needed anything. She decided on an early
night herself. She knew that Gary would be at the casino
and there was nothing to stop her going too, yet somehow
she had no heart for it tonight.

When the sun shines down from a clear blue sky all the
fears of the night seem to fly with the darkness. With roses
tumbling in scented clouds, tiny button flowers in the trees,
lush tropical blossom and palm tree greenery mirrored in
the pool the atmosphere at Koudia righted itself the next
morning as though the spirits of those within its walls were
touched, uplifted by the vigour of growing things.

Breakfast on the little terrace with its view of the Casbah
rooftops and sparkling sea was almost a merry affair. Summer was upon them, and as though there wasn't enough

colour to strike at the heart with its beauty, a gay sun
umbrella had been erected to soften the glare. Robert looking rested, his over-long blond thatch endearing him to
Vivienne, actually ate most of his special breakfast bran that
was prepared for him. Trent was wearing the kind of summer outfit, patterned beach shirt and linen slacks, which
highlighted his tan and the premature grey at his temples.
She thought, as he looked at her from time to time across
the table, that his eyes had never looked bluer. For some
reason she felt like singing inside. There was a strange kind
of perfection about the morning just sitting here like this,
with Trent and Robert.

After breakfast she pushed the wheelchair along the
paths through the grounds and she and Robert laughed at
the antics of a puppy who belonged to one of the Berber
workmen spraying the fruit trees. They spent the afternoon
in the pool, tusselling for the inflated armchairs and grimac-
ing hilariously when the chlorinated water slopped into
their drinks. Vivienne felt at one with the blue sky and the
lush green surroundings. If only life could go on like this!
If only Robert ... Swiftly she stifled the ache in her and
laughingly lunged with him for a beach ball.

She didn't think about her rendezvous with Gary until
she was changing for dinner that evening. She had rested
after Robert had retired to his own rooms and later showered away the pool water and covered herself liberally with
a sweet-smelling cologne. Now, padding over the carpet in
bare feet and a cool lace slip, she pondered on what to wear.
She didn't possess a large wardrobe, but she had always
shopped carefully when buying clothes, preferring to settle
for one really good dress rather than several cheap separ-
ates. She was glad of this now because the casino attracted
a considerable number of the dilettante type who dressed
expensively and it was nice to know she wouldn't be letting
Trent down by her appearance.

She chose a dress of soft magnolia pink with a silver
thread in it. It had a neat stand-up collar and small cap
sleeves and she thought the slim skirt and wide silver belt

gave her a chic appearance. She fastened a tiny silver star in her hair at each side so that it was drawn back a little from her face. She was so tanned now that make-up was hardly necessary, but a touch of powder took the shine off her skin and a shell-pink lipstick gave warmth to her colouring and brought out the hazel lights in her eyes. She had no silver shoes, unfortunately, but her rose-pink sandals with the neat slim heels seemed just right with her sun-tanned legs.

Trent was waiting downstairs in the room where they dined. He let his glance roam over her as she came to the table but made no comment as he eased her chair in. They talked leisurely through the meal, mostly about the events of the day. Trent had been in his usual place at the poolside during the afternoon and was content as she was that Robert had had a good session. It wasn't until they were on the sweet and he was passing her a dish of jellied cherries that he remarked suavely on her appearance. 'You're looking very attractive tonight, Vivienne. Do I take it you're planning another visit to the casino?'

'Do you mind?' She served herself and handed him back the dish.

'Not at all.' He gave her a lazy smile. 'It's good for you to enjoy a little company occasionally. And I'd prefer it was at the Café Anglais than some other night spot.'

After the meal they adjourned to the window area. The nights were warm now and he led the way through an open doorway to a small elevated space entwined with creepers and vines. They smoked their cigarettes in silence, both gazing towards the twinkling lights of the city and listening to the distant sound of the Atlantic breakers on the shore. When Trent turned to go in it was well past his usual time for starting out to the casino.

Vivienne left him in the hall and went to her room to touch up her make-up and generally prepare for the evening. She heard the car go as she was dabbing a little perfume at her wrists and ear lobes. It was a few minutes before ten when she came downstairs. She was about to go in search of the manservant to tell him she would require the car when Trent appeared. Luckily she was able to contain her surprise. As he approached he said easily, 'I sent Abdul on ahead to keep his eye on things. I thought I might as well drive you down myself, seeing that we're both going to the same place.'

'Fine!' Vivienne agreed lightly, but her heart was thudding as he led her out to his car. Trent had never accompanied her to the casino before. His proximity in the gloom made her blazingly conscious of her promise to Gary to meet him there.

They were using the wine-coloured racer. She thought that Trent, groomed in white dinner jacket and finely creased dark trousers, was more suited to the elegant limousine when dressed like this, though he slid into the seat behind the wheel blending in with the expensive crampedness of the interior, gold-studded shirt cuffs and all.

The town was packed with people, dining out, strolling the streets, sitting in the crowded sidewalk cafés or on their way to one of the many cabarets where the rhythm of the tambourines and undulating torsos of girl dancers attracted a great number of visitors. Trent had to drive at a snail's pace in some places, and the position wasn't much better when they arrived at the casino. He paid a watchman to keep an eye on his car and guided Vivienne down to the sea front.

Outside the Café Anglais, there was a sizeable group of Moroccans in rough-looking garb and their mood, judging by the noise, was argumentative. Vivienne felt Trent's hand on her arm tighten. He drew her close to him as they made to pass inside. They had reached the forecourt where tubbed oleanders perfumed the night and the lights spilled out from within. Then everything seemed to happen at once. There was a cry from one of the robed figures and a scuffle broke out. En masse the knot of pushing, grappling bodies surged this way and that demolishing everything in its path. Tubs went over and though they were almost at the door Vivienne winced as her shin was scraped by some jutting object. Trent cursed and ushered her before him shouldering off the worst of it and giving the brawlers the benefit of his tongue in vitriolic Arabic.

They almost fell inside and Trent, straightening himself, his hair and dinner jacket awry, steadied Vivienne with a hand. 'Are you all right?' He looked at her shin with her and she laughed it off, seeing that only the skin was broken. 'It's nothing.'

By the time they had brushed themselves off the forecourt was empty and the disturbance had passed on. Trent thrust a hand into his pocket and gave her the keys to his office, 'Go in and clean up. I'll be along as soon as I've got someone to tidy things up here.'

Vivienne went through the café. No one had noticed their somewhat hectic entrance and she was able to move between the tables with a comparatively serene air. She was becoming used to the smiling acknowledgement of the staff and rather liked the atmosphere of bonhomie that prevailed for her benefit. In the palm-lined vestibule she was greeted by the Oriental bows from the turbanned casino attendants. She walked past the archways which looked on to the gaming rooms and let herself into Trent's office. In the small adjoining cloakroom she sponged her shin at the washbasin and smoothed her dress and her hair, obliterating all signs of the skirmish.

When Trent came in she was examining an old framed map of Tangier which hung on the wall above the divan. He went to the cloakroom himself and washed his hands, and coming out drying them he asked with a grin, 'Still in one piece?'

'We were lucky to have somewhere to retreat to,' she said with a laugh, and glancing down at her tanned legs, 'I can't even claim damages for a new pair of tights.' Her shin bone was showing a small violet bruise.

Trent went to the cupboard above the washbasin and brought out a tin of ointment. 'This will ease it.'

She sat on the divan and he crouched beside her gently smearing cream over the bruise. She noticed the way the lapels of his dinner jacket were tugged open at his shirt front by the muscular width of his shoulders; the liquid-black shine of his shoes and the bronze lights in his hair.

When he rose to his feet his expression had lapsed a little grim. 'After tonight I'm having second thoughts about you coming down here to the casino in the evenings.'

'But why?' She stood up beside him. 'A grazed leg's nothing.'

'I don't like the idea of you being mixed up in the kind of rough-house we had just now.' He replaced the ointment in the cupboard. 'At this time of the year there's all kinds of types drifting down from the hills and the open country-side. They come looking for work and to sell hand-made goods, and the money they earn sometimes goes to their heads.'

'I'm sure tonight was just an isolated incident,' Vivienne remarked cheerfully.

'Maybe,' Trent nodded. 'But the port attracts the troublemakers, and a percentage of them are bound to find their way into the casino. We've already had a couple of unpleasant episodes and there could be more. I don't want a woman in my family mixed up in it.' He went over to the bar and poured two drinks and Vivienne accepted hers not knowing what else to say on the matter.

A few minutes later the various heads of staff started making their appearance to confer with Trent on procedure for the evening. Vivienne finished her drink and said in an aside, 'I'll get out of your way. There's bound to be some-thing of interest going on at one of the gaming tables.'

He came to the door with her and looked her over with a smile. 'Sure the leg's okay?'

She nodded and tripping past him replied, 'I've already forgotten about it.' The door closed behind her and she wandered leisurely with no particular purpose in mind. It was early yet and the gaming rooms were still comparatively empty. She strolled through to the bar in the café and sat on one of the tall stools to pass the time. She was becoming known here now. One of the waiters, a swarthy good-natured type from the Iberian peninsula, joked with her as waiters will. He was surprised and delighted to discover that she could chat away in Spanish. They had an interesting conversation, mainly about his family, half of whom lived in Algeciras and the other half in Gibraltar, and how their only way of communication was to meet at the wire netting barrier and throw things over to one another. Vivienne left when business brisked up and people were waiting for seats at the bar.

The gaming rooms were lively when she returned, although by no means up to their usual capacity. She drifted in and joined the punters at one of the tables to watch the game. She wasn't thinking of Gary, and when a voice at her side said, 'Hi! I've been waiting for you,' her immediate reaction was one of alarm. She said in low tones, 'I thought you were going to wait until the place had filled up.'

'It's all right,' he replied as though extremely interested in the layout of the chips on the table. 'We'll find a table hidden away somewhere in the café, where we can talk.'

He gave her a gentle push in that direction and she found herself preceding him and nervously telling herself that of course it was all right. She was on smiling terms now with many of the regulars. Didn't it follow that sooner or later someone would ask her to join them in a drink? Having convinced herself that she was worrying unnecessarily, she sauntered across the vestibule alongside Gary and through into the café, negligently searching with him for a suitable table. They found one beyond a far archway where a fringed lampshade cast shadows into the corner. Gary had ordered and he waited until two long drinks had been placed on their table. When they were alone he took her hand in his across the table. 'Darling, it's good to see you again. I felt hellish rushing off and leaving you like that the other day. Am I forgiven?'

Whether it was the nervous tension that had numbed her a little Vivienne couldn't have said. She only knew that she felt slightly dazed at Gary's rather hearty greeting. 'Well, of course!' She gave a jerky laugh. 'You explained that you had to get back to work. I didn't think any more of it.'

'Does that mean you haven't been thinking of me?' He looked hurt and squeezed her hand. 'I've been counting the hours until I could see you again. And now we have to do it like this. Bit of a hole-and-corner affair, isn't it?'

Vivienne's tones were full of remorse. 'I'm sorry, Gary. I did explain the position. I thought you understood that Robert——'

'Don't get me wrong,' a crooked smile quickly appeared on his lips. 'I don't mind fitting in with things if it will help the sick youngster. It's just that I'm longing to take you in my arms, and all I can do is offer you a drink.'

Vivienne's senses were in a whirl. The moment she had waited for for four long years was here. Gary wanted her back. She wanted to feel the joy, the glow she had lived through time and time again whenever she had pictured this moment. Instead her emotions were strung-up, over-taut in some way. Perhaps it had all happened too suddenly. Perhaps the worry over Robert was dulling the sweetness—she didn't know. All she could see in her mind was the picture of Trent crouched beside the divan rubbing cream over her bruised shin. She laughed to dispel the picture and consoled Gary, 'Never mind. Think of it as adding a spice of excitement to our meetings.'

'Do we need that?' She must have looked mildly at a loss at his fervency, for he added, gaily changing the subject, 'Tell me all about your search. Uncanny how you knew I'd still be here in Tangier.'

'Well, it was funny. I went to all our usual haunts ...' Vivienne sipped her drink and explained how she had combed the Casbah and the old town and wandered around the city blocks and parks, and all the time she had the feeling that Gary wasn't listening. When she had finished he said briefly, squeezing her hand again, 'Not to worry. We're together now, and that's all that matters.'

They had been sitting for a good twenty minutes and

looking round worriedly Vivienne said, 'Hadn't we better be getting back to the gaming rooms?'

'I've got a better idea.' A few tables along a grilled doorway was open on to the night. As she rose Gary ushered her before him out into the shadows.

They were in what was obviously the casino gardens. The air was scented with lemon trees and tall palms waved their fronds against the dark sky. The lap and swish of the sea could be heard from round the front of the building. Gary drew her into his arms and placed his lips on hers before she had time to get used to the gloom, and kept them there. He paused briefly to murmur against her, 'This is more like it. Now it's like old times again.'

Gary holding her close! How often she had imagined this moment. She ought to be melting in his arms, giving him kiss for kiss, yet all she could do was strain a look towards the lights from the gaming room windows and whisper uneasily, 'We'd better be careful, Gary. Someone might see us.'

'There's no one about at this time of night,' he replied, not slackening his hold. 'You get the elderly types strolling round in the afternoon, but nobody come out here in the dark.' He kissed her lingeringly and firmly and she made an effort to forget the indoors. It seemed an age to her before he finally released her and they started to walk. She longed to turn and go back inside, yet she didn't know how to suggest it to Gary without appearing abrupt. When he spoke she discovered oddly enough that he too was mindful of the dangers. 'We'll have to be careful of our meetings,' he said, standing and looking thoughtful. 'Luckily we're safe out here. And we can always give each other the eye inside.'

Vivienne shook her head. 'I'm not sure I'm going to be able to come to the casino, Gary. Trent was saying earlier tonight that he didn't think it was a good idea. There was some trouble at the doorway when we arrived. He talked as though he'd changed his mind about allowing me to spend the evenings here.'

'Do you think he suspects something?' Gary asked, shooting her a look.

'I'm not sure.' She bit her lip worriedly. And thinking back over all her uncertain moments with Trent she shook her head and said on a note of despair, 'I wish I knew!' They walked a little and she added reflectively, 'I sometimes think he suspects I'm not as much in love with Robert as I make out to be.'

Gary kicked his feet along the path for a while, then turned to give her a smile. 'You're probably imagining things. I expect it's all okay. And we're not going to do anything to upset things. We'll go inside now, and split up straightaway. And don't worry, my sweet, I don't mind playing along.' He hugged her to him and she felt obliged to tell him,

'You're an angel, Gary. It's good of you to understand.'

Relief washed over her once they were back inside the café. In the shadows she moved alone and emerged over near the bar. A little later she went to the gaming rooms. Time had flown and the place was crowded. She drifted about for a while, but the sparkle the evening seemed to have had earlier had vanished. Her clandestine meeting with Gary had given her an edgy feeling. She wanted only to get back to Koudia.

Trent was engaged in conversation with a group near the casino bar. Vivienne didn't know whether he had seen her or not. At the baccarat table she watched a dowager figure who was doing rather well. The plump old lady wore black velvet and a glittering tiara and looked considerably incongruous sandwiched between a Texan-styled gentleman in a ten-gallon hat and an Arab in camel-hair headgear. Vivienne was taking a mild interest in the way the woman's chips were mounting when Trent came over to join her.

'Our best client,' he said in low tones, nodding at the dowager. 'She's got a fairly workable system and sticks to it.'

'But don't you mind her coming and winning like that?' Vivienne asked with an incredulous laugh.

'Not at all.' He took her arm. 'She's a good advertisement for the place. Nobody gets excited about a loser.'

'And they're not all mathematical geniuses,' Vivienne remarked mischievously.

'Precisely,' he smiled succinctly as they moved away.

When they had drifted between the tables for a moment or two she said casually, 'I know you rely on Abdul rather at this time of night, but I wonder if you could spare him to drive me home.'

Trent stopped to run his gaze over her. 'Not still shaky, are you? Leg troubling you?'

'No, of course not,' she smiled. 'It's just that the crowds are a bit overwhelming and it is quite late.' She wished she could sound more convincing, and was it her imagination or was his gaze unusually searching as she made her excuses? She thought she would give herself away, then he said, moving his glance on at last, 'Abdul was here a moment ago. I'll go and find him.'

He returned before she had time to still her thumping heart. Abdul gave her his polite salaam. 'I've explained that you want to be driven straight home,' Trent told her. She thanked him and said goodnight. As she left him and made her way through to the café she knew that his gaze stayed trained on her until she was out of sight.

CHAPTER SEVEN

ROBERT had another collapse the following day. Vivienne had been swimming with him and suddenly his eyes closed and he sank like a stone. Haroun dived in and brought him to the side, brushing the wet hair from his face and crooning to him as though he was a child. Vivienne wanted to burst into tears, but Trent's white, taut features made her forget herself. She helped him to wrap Robert in his towelling robe and went up with him to his room, while Trent phoned for the doctor.

The house dropped very quiet. The servants moved about on slippered feet and no one spoke. No sound came from the kitchens where Maurice the chef could normally be heard carolling tunes from the French operas as he moved back and forth from his ovens. At last the doctors left, and after a reasonable lapse of time Vivienne went up to the top floor suite in the left wing. She found Robert sitting up in bed. His skin had a yellowish pallor, but he was smiling and seemed like his old self. Trent had relaxed a little. He suggested that they all have dinner in his brother's room, and when the table was set and the candles were lit and they were all three sat facing the spangled view of the city, the nightmare day might never have been. Vivienne said a small prayer before she went to bed that night.

Robert came out to breakfast as usual the next morning. It seemed that his doctors saw no sense in him lying in bed in his room when summer was making itself felt everywhere in the grounds. Vivienne was relieved to hear this. Although the views from the top of the house were uplifting and cheerful she knew that Robert loved the outdoors.

During the morning she pushed him along his favourite

stroll round the grounds and in the afternoon they played croquet. For once Trent joined in the game. He left his briefcase and his business books on the table by the pool and strolled over to take his turn with the mallet. Vivienne didn't play quite so well with him looking on, but she didn't mind that. Robert was delighted to have the opportunity of pitting himself against his brother and she was quite happy to let the game develop into a two-sided affair. Watching Trent and his younger brother battle it out good-humouredly gave her a warm kind of satisfaction, far more than she would have got from trying to compete with one or the other of them herself.

At the end of the game, which had finished in a tight draw, they all retired to the clump of olive trees at the far end of the lawned strip where comfortable loungers were spread in the shade. Haroun, who had had the tricky job of manoeuvring the wheelchair over the course, went to put the mallets away and to cool off. Robert's face glistened, and Vivienne knew he was very tired. She dabbed his brow soothingly with a tissue and pushed his shaggy blond hair from his brow. She hadn't reckoned on him having any spare energy at that moment and was taken unawares when he turned his arms round her waist and pulled her down to him. She was wearing only a thin summer dress with the minimum of underwear beneath and she guessed that his touch had discovered this.

'You're cool and sweet-smelling, like one of those wood flowers.' He trailed a finger through a tendril of her hair and smiled. 'You know what you remind me of? The lily of the valley.' He gazed at the sky as though for inspiration and said, looking into her eyes, 'Nothing comes to mind on those lines at the moment, but how about this—*I cannot see what flowers are at my feet, nor what soft incense hangs upon the boughs ...*'

Vivienne stirred where she rested against him. She always felt ill at ease when he quoted poetry at her, though she knew that often it was the only way he could express his feelings. She wished she possessed a similar sensitivity to reply, but she wasn't Lucy and she guessed that he felt a sense of let-down at her lack of response to his romantic prose. She felt doubly awkward just now with Trent there organising drinks at the table. Hoping to gloss over the bad moment, she poked Robert playfully in the ribs and rising to her feet told him, 'I think it's about time I cut your hair.'

Along with her he accepted a glass from Trent and flicking a wryly humorous look her way he asked his brother, 'Do you think women are changing, Trent? There was a time when they'd swoon at the thought of soft guitars and someone making lyrical noises in their ear. Now what have we got? I whisper words of pure gold to my girl and she tells me I need a haircut!'

Vivienne looked at her drink rather than at Trent. Never did she feel she was walking on thin ice more than on these occasions when her identity was in question. She heard him reply lazily, 'Could be that Vivienne's not on your wavelength when it comes to the bards and their works, old man.'

Her look flew to his then. Was he guessing or did he know? As always his sky-blue eyes gave nothing away. Robert was saying, 'You're wrong, Trent. Viv's very poetic at heart. When we were writing to each other we used to end most of our letters in verse.'

She put in hastily, though professing a casual air, 'What no one seems to realise is that the poets are all right in their place, but we girls are concerned with flesh and blood, not some musty and ancient past. Writing letters is one thing, but when you've got that special person close to you,' she hinted at Robert with her smile, 'who needs Keats or Browning to tell you how to behave?'

He clasped her wrist and drew her cheek down to his and looking at Trent he joked, 'Do you think it's the Tangier air that's got her talking all matter-of-fact?'

'I reckon that's it, Rob,' Trent drawled in reply. Vivienne's glance met his and though she thought she had covered herself rather well, she couldn't be sure with Trent.

She straightened and took a drink from her glass. That was it. With Trent she could never be sure.

The days were almost carefree, despite the fact that Robert had suffered another relapse and was not up to his usual vitality. Vivienne spent all her time with him, leaving him only in the evenings when he needed to rest. In her room she wrote long letters to Lucy. It was upsetting to have to tell her of Robert's failing strength, but she knew that her friend would wish to know the truth and so she reported faithfully all that happened.

The nights were warm and laced with the sandalwood scent of the Levant. She would sit with her doors open so that the faint clamour could be heard rising from the city. Trent had never actually forbidden her to go to the casino, yet she had no desire to exchange the peace of Koudia for the outdoors. After dinner, when she had been upstairs to see that Robert had everything for his comfort for the night, she would tell Abdul that she wouldn't be requiring his services and later he would leave for the casino where he was needed. She had grown quite used to amusing herself alone in the big luxurious house.

One evening she had washed her hair and was sitting in her room reading a book she had brought up from the library, when an odd noise attracted her attention. It sounded like a rattling on the glass at the windows. She went to see if a breeze was springing up, thinking that perhaps the catches were rattling, but all was still and quiet over by the balcony. She hadn't read more than a few lines after going back to her chair when the noise came again. This time she was sure it couldn't be her imagination.

Putting down her book, she went out on to the wide balcony that ran the length of the upstairs rooms and looked over. All was dark down there, then her heart leapt into her throat as she saw a moving shape. Before she had time to react she heard a voice say softly, 'It's all right. It's me, Gary.'

Gary—here! Vivienne let out a horrified gasp and ran

quickly down the flight of stairs at the side. He came up a short way to meet her. In the darkness she could see his smile. 'I was wondering when you'd hear the pebbles at the window. I guessed it was your room. It's the only one lit at the front.'

She looked about wildly and said in agonised undertones, 'Gary, you shouldn't have come here.'

'It's okay, I checked first.' He made to draw her into his arms. 'The house is all quiet. There's no one about.'

'But there are servants,' she cried beneath her breath. And they might be spotted from the outdoors too. The villa was filled with precious antiques. She knew that Trent employed watchmen to patrol the grounds. What if one of them should happen along now? She racked her brain nervously, then had an idea. The *minzah*! No one would see them there. 'Come on,' she dragged him down the steps, 'I know a place.'

He allowed her to lead him through the darkness, moving through the mimosa thicket and along the path to the ruined pavilion, with a carefree, unhurried step that irritated her. She worried about the noisy fluttering of the birds as they stumbled into the tumbledown doorway, convinced that they were making enough din to attract the whole night-watch force. She was listening with palpitating heart when Gary drew her into his arms and forced his lips on hers. She was so agitated she wanted to push him away, but his embrace was unyielding, almost as if she had no choice in the matter, and after a while she calmed down and made an effort to focus her attention on his kiss.

Her senses were still linked with the outside and the house and her neck was beginning to ache. She had never thought she would feel annoyance at Gary's prolonged love-making. It was the fact that he seemed to be wielding some kind of monopoly that angered her, and though it was the reverse of the way she had always dreamed it, she broke away from his kiss.

Gary seemed not to notice any strain. He kept a hold on her and murmured, 'You smell like a Sultan's lady all powdered and ready for the harem. Your hair's damp and perfumed.'

'I've just washed it.' She tried not to sound short, telling herself it was absurd to be cross with Gary simply because he had been enterprising enough to figure out a way to see her.

He was saying close to her cheek, 'I made a couple of trips up here in the afternoon. It was easy knowing where to find you once I got the layout of the orchards and the house.'

Vivienne listened appalled. She said none too gently, 'You shouldn't wander around here in broad daylight, Gary. It's very risky.'

'Don't worry, I made sure nobody saw me.' His grin seemed a trifle hard in the gloom, then he pulled her close to him. 'I'm not sorry you've had to give the town a miss. This is much better than the casino.'

'But dare we meet here, Gary? So close to the house?' She covered her alarm with reasonable tones. 'I think it might be wiser to wait a few days. I'm sure a better arrangement will offer itself.'

'We'll see.' His lips were searching for hers and she felt bound to acquiesce to his demands. But just when she was telling herself firmly that this was Gary and that she should be making the most of their being alone together like this, he let her go and began to move restlessly about the interior. She told him something about the history of the *minzah* and they stood and watched the clouds sailing across the starlit sky through one of the arched window apertures. It seemed to her that his attention was wandering to other things, and after a while he said, 'I suppose I'd better go. You might be missed at the house and I want to be seen around at the casino.'

Vivienne had no idea what he meant by this last part of his remark and she didn't stop to wonder. She was too concerned with seeing him off the grounds and getting back to her room before anyone discovered them to bother with last-minute chat.

Out in the darkness she told him in a whisper, 'There's a quick way down into the orchards on the other side of the mimosa.'

'Don't worry, I know my way. I'll get out on to the road all right.' He gripped her suddenly and planted his lips on hers, then with a departing wave he called, ' 'Bye, my sweet. And keep your chin up. Everything's going to be all right!'

He disappeared, and she hurried back towards the house. It took her several minutes battling with the lower branches along the route which kept snarling her dressing gown, and at one point her blood froze when, shattering the stillness, came the excited barking of a dog. The puppy belonging to the tree workers, a leggy creature by now, was chained down by the sheds at the foot of the slopes, and it was from here where the racket ensued. Vivienne held her breath, expecting the worst, but after a while the barking settled down. There was a friendly whine and one or two delighted yelps, then silence. Wilting with relief, she ran the rest of the way to the house.

She had intended to get back to her room by the outside stairway and was just coming round from the side of the house, when the lights along the lower archways sprang on and Momeen appeared on the front steps. 'Mademoiselle!' His eyes popped in his olive-skinned features as he looked about him. 'Is everything all right? I heard noises. Where are those stupid watchmen?' His pantaloons and waistcoat were awry and he had obviously stirred himself from the comforts of an armchair to see what the fuss was about.

'I thought I heard something too,' Vivienne strove to give the impression of having just come out. She waved an arm and smiled. 'I expect it's just the town youths playing games near the gates. Nothing to worry about.' She changed her mind about the side stairway now and wandering casually indoors climbed the hall staircase and called, 'All's quiet now. Goodnight, Momeen.'

He gave her an uncertain salaam and whispered away in his slippered feet to his own quarters.

Vivienne hardly slept that night and the following day,

was one of the worst she had known since arriving at Koudia, when she had been foolish enough to believe she could pass herself off as Lucy Miles. She lived through the meals in an agony of suspense, sure that at any moment Momeen was going to come out with a colourful description of the disturbance that had taken place the night before. Nor could she relax near the pool or on the croquet pitch, for each time she lifted her gaze she had a horrible dread of seeing Gary appear along one of the garden paths.

She knew that Trent watched her. She was pale with nerves and though she laughed a lot and was more than usually active she couldn't shake off her edginess. She hoped he would put it down to the strain of Robert's wavering health. It was a minor disaster when the young invalid expressed a desire to skip dinner and go straight to bed. That meant that she would have to dine alone with Trent downstairs. She would have liked to plead tiredness too, but was afraid that this might draw attention to her nerviness, so she bathed and changed as usual for dinner.

The evening was hot and in a sleeveless dress of coffee-coloured silk, her hair caught back with the star-slides for coolness, Vivienne went downstairs determined to see the rest of the day through somehow. She would have preferred it if Trent had been late and she could have seen herself to the table, but unluckily he was there as usual, groomed and dressed for the casino, and she felt his eyes on her as he held her chair. They were barely through the soup course when he said, dropping all pretence at polite conversation, 'Aren't you feeling well? You've been looking close to breaking point all day.'

Alarm coursed through her, but she smiled and replied off-handedly, 'I'm fine. Just a little tired, perhaps.'

Trent frowned. 'If Rob's wearing you out, you should tell him so. He's still pretty powerful in the water, and he's inclined to forget that for a girl it's much tougher to keep up.'

She couldn't think of a suitable reply and, afraid that he might follow up with more probing, she said a little hurriedly, 'I've often thought that your brother needs something more than ... well, Koudia. I mean, I know he's got the magnificent pool and you've had the croquet pitch installed, and then he's got all his indoor hobbies, but it is, after all, a narrow world for someone of his age.'

'I've tried to encourage Rob to have more young people at the house, but this is something you'd have to take up with him,' Trent said tersely. 'Although we don't notice it I've a hunch they might make him feel too conscious of his affliction.'

'Oh, I wasn't thinking so much of *people*,' Vivienne commented, the idea that was forming in her mind gathering momentum. 'I meant ... well, a change of scene. That is if he were strong enough to take to the suggestion.'

Trent was thoughtful. 'Rob makes the journey to the hospital every week,' he pointed out, and added with a shrug, 'A few miles wouldn't affect him, though he's never shown any desire to spend his time anywhere but at Koudia.'

'But think what it would do for him, Trent.' Vivienne leaned across the table. 'Do you know that Robert told me he's never been on an island. Surely that's not such a tall order? And I'm convinced the break would do him good.'

Trent was eyeing her curiously and she realised she was pressing for his agreement a little too fervently. He said, without moving his gaze from her flushed cheeks and over-bright eyes, 'There's Tahad Island, just across Tangier bay. It's private property, but I know the owner. I think I could persuade him to loan me his summer house there.'

'It sounds ideal,' Vivienne prattled on recklessly now. 'Robert wouldn't be bothered with people, and small islands are better. It would really be something new for him. I'm sure he'll like the idea.'

'I'm sure he will, when you put it to him,' Trent said drily.

She was too keyed up to think much about the rest of the meal, and when they rose at the end of it she asked, trying to play down her eagerness, 'This friend of yours who owns the island—will you be seeing him soon?'

'Tonight, I should think,' Trent replied. 'He's a regular visitor to the casino.'

'Does that mean,' she held her breath, 'we could get away fairly quickly?'

Holding her chair, he asked lazily, though she knew that he was watching her closely, 'How soon would you want to get away?'

'Oh, tomorrow!' The idea was such a good one she was past caring now what Trent thought. 'We could talk to Robert at breakfast and if he's happy about it—I know he will be—start out soon after lunch. Do you think we could?'

Trent said with his dry gleam, 'I think it could be arranged.'

'In that case,' she gave him a bright smile before whirling away, 'I'll go upstairs now and sort out a few things to pack.'

She heard the car go and later while she was going through her drawers she thought about Robert, more than ever convinced that the trip was what he needed. If he hadn't got much time left shouldn't he do all the exciting things he could manage before ... before ... Well, it didn't do to look too far ahead.

As it happened he was in the same adventurous frame of mind when she put it to him enthusiastically the next morning, especially when he heard there was a natural sea-water pool on the island and their own private beach. Trent told them that it was all fixed up and by mid-afternoon they were settled in at Tahad Island, having made the journey of no more than a dozen miles round the bay to the far headland, where a private boat had been waiting. Though they could see the tall white blocks of Tangier in the distance and even Koudia, a small speck on the rise above, they might have been in another world, cut off as they were with the green-blue sea all around them and low umbrella pines and carpets of wild flowers close at hand. The beach was a long tongue of golden sand at the farthest tip of the tiny island.

All was activity indoors, everyone cheerfully tolerant of the fact that the mademoiselle had taken it into her head to whisk them away from the mansion on the hillside to this remote spot in the middle of the ocean. Maurice had been persuaded to come and sang excerpts from *La Bohème* in stentorian tones while preparing the evening meal. Momeen aired bed linen and rubbed up the kitchen silver and Abdul went around in a supervisory capacity, apparently doing little but as always keeping everything running with its customary smoothness.

The house, like the beach, looked out on to the straits of Gibraltar. It lacked the grandness of Koudia, but Vivienne liked its spacious uncluttered rooms and wide-windowed views. The floors were of pale glossy tiles, covered with skin rugs, and the furnishings, tall glass-fronted cupboards in primrose wood, pale leather upholstery and bright chintz armchairs. There were several guest rooms, a large lounge with expensive but simple comforts, and an elevated glass-screened patio, for outdoor or indoor dining.

When Robert had rested and all the unpacking was done they went down to explore the beach. The sun was gloriously hot and the breeze blowing in from the open sea, salt-tanged and bracing.

It was soon discovered that wheelchairs are not made to be pushed over soft sand, and some thinking had to be done to devise a way to give Robert free passage to and from the house. While Haroun went to scout for tough bracken that would give a firm base when dug in Trent mapped out a walk along the edge of the sea. It seemed strange to see him in checked shirt and shorts, his hair ruffled, and a russet glow on his tanned face as he worked in the face of the breeze.

Vivienne helped him to plan the most picturesque route and later to dig in the bracken flooring. They made a walk around the entire jutting strip of beach. It was an ambitious project and she felt shattered when it was completed. Robert was surprisingly full of vitality and impish humour since his arrival and couldn't wait to sample the road his menials had made for him, and enlisted Haroun, still brushing the sand from his knees, to take him on a grand tour.

Trent came to drop down where Vivienne had collapsed on the sand as the two departed. She was staring out to sea, the laughter still on her lips, breathing in the delicious freedom of the place. He said with cryptic humour, 'Happier now that Rob's got his island?'

She thought of Koudia closed up and deserted with only the watchmen patrolling the grounds, and nodded. Yes, she was content.

After they had sat for a while gazing to where the boisterous Atlantic met the placid Mediterranean Trent drawled, 'You'll find a parcel in your room. As this is a kind of holiday I figured you'd need some beach gear for the occasion.'

Vivienne turned to rest her smiling eyes on him. 'A present? For me?'

He shrugged with a grin, 'You threatened to go threadbare on us, remember. I thought for everyone's peace of mind we'd better do something about that one and only swimsuit.'

Vivienne's lips twitched. She remembered the fight she had had with Trent over her bikini. It seemed a long way in the past now. They hadn't had a skirmish for some time. She lowered her lashes and said demurely, 'Well, thank you.'

The wheelchair was returning, and waving excitedly but with some little frustration, Robert called, 'Hey, you should see the birds back there in the woods behind the rocks! It's like a zoo aviary. And what prize nit forgot to pack his field glasses!'

'Relax,' said Trent, rising to his feet. 'I brought them. They're in the house.'

Vivienne went back with Robert to bird-watch where the pines grew down to the rocky edge across on the far side of the beach, so that it was sunset before she was able to open the parcel in her room. She found a couple of expensive swimsuits patterned in exotic Indian designs, a striped shorts-and-bra beach outfit and two embroidered shortie caftans. They were lovely garments and Trent must have a trained eye for measurements, where she was concerned at any rate, for every one fitted perfectly. When they were re-folded again on the bed, these bright new assets to her wardrobe, she looked at them and suddenly felt the glisten of tears in her eyes. Which was foolish indeed, she told herself.

They dined informally on the spacious patio with the glass screens drawn back and the waves washing restfully over the rocks almost at their feet. The scent of juniper, tamarisk and pine mingled with the strong, warm odour of the sea and the night was black beyond the windows with nothing to remind them of the civilisation that lay behind them on the mainland.

Robert had stayed up to have dinner with them, and Vivienne was touched by the sight of him, his blue eyes, so like Trent's, aglow with the novelty of the adventure, his flaxen hair tousled and smelling of the sea. He was talkative too and while he rattled away to Trent about what they had seen during the afternoon she thought, more than a little pleased with herself, that the break from Koudia had truly given him something new to think about.

Haroun came to wheel him away to his room just after nine. Vivienne sat on one of the settees in the comfortable lounge and flicked through a magazine. Trent, in an arm-chair across from her, seemed absorbed in the book he had chosen for himself from the packed shelves. She thought he would have gone off to change for the casino before this. They were only fifteen minutes by boat away from the mainland and barely the same again by car from the city.

Around ten he closed the book and said with a wry smile, 'I've a nasty suspicion that all Tom Harris's novels are who-dunnits.'

Turning the pages of her magazine, Vivienne joked, 'Per-haps he thinks the island is the ideal setting for that kind of reading.'

'It's also a good spot to get lost in a rip-roaring saga of the sea, if I could find one,' said Trent, eyeing the book-shelves but making little effort to rise.

Vivienne asked then, 'Aren't you going to the Café Anglais?'

His answer was to relax back further into his chair. Then he replied, 'I've left Raymond in charge of the gaming tables. And Abdul knows the office routine. He'll be making the nightly trip in my place.'

Vivienne looked at the glossy photographs and news items before her without seeing them. She became acutely conscious of the quiet of the house and the fitful sigh of the sea breezes gently buffeting the windows. She thought Trent might have offered her a cigarette, she could have done with something just then, but he sat, or so it seemed to her, looking down at his shoes. She turned the pages of her magazine, conscious of their dry crackle as the silence stretched between them, then Trent said, 'Like to go for a walk on the beach?'

She rose with him and said brightly, 'That would be nice.'

It was just light enough to see the path by the blaze of stars. The sea spilled in from the darkness leaving frills of foam at their feet. They walked along its edge, neither say-ing a word as their shoes crunched in slow rhythm over the sand, as the wind sighed softly out at sea. They walked the entire stretch round the projection of beach, then they said goodnight and went to their rooms.

The days that followed at the island retreat had a magic holiday flavour. They borrowed a small boat and Trent carried his brother aboard piggy-back style amidst joking comments, and took them on picturesque excursions round the island alongside rock pools and bird sanctuaries. They swam in the sea-water pool, a charming hideaway at the side of the house screened by palms and cascading greenery and dotted with giant makebelieve waterlilies. And not content with this, Robert swam in the sea too, ducking

Vivienne and punching a ball to Trent, and dragging himself out mainly by his hands when he felt like it to flop out laughingly on the beach.

Lying alongside him in the hot sun, Vivienne would try not to notice his dwindling frame, or if she did she would tell herself, with a tightness in her throat, that at least he was getting the utmost out of the days that were left to him. He made the trip to the hospital in his usual unfussy way, insisting that he needed no one except Abdul to accompany him. Vivienne took advantage of his absence to wash the salt water out of her hair and later stretched out on a sun bed where the shade of pines softened the view of beach and sky. Trent flicked through the daily newspaper nearby.

They all grew very brown with the open air life they were leading, the ruggedness of sea and sand landscape contrasting considerably with the formal luxury of Koudia. Trent developed a weathered look, his hair sandy and windblown as he helped Robert to cast a fishing line, his teeth strong and white against the ruddy glow of his face as he shipped the boat in at sunset.

Vivienne found herself wishing that life could stay suspended like this, for Robert too; that they could all three go on just as they were with no interference from the outside world. With the long summer days and nights when the sky was jewelled with stars it certainly seemed that nothing could break the spell.

She spoke her thoughts to Trent one evening when the beauty of the night awoke in her a sudden rush of words. They were standing looking at the moonlit sea from the front steps of the house and it had grown very late. 'It's all so perfect,' Vivienne rested back against a vine and sighed. 'It doesn't seem possible that there could be anything to mar such contentment.' But there was. They both knew there was. She didn't know why she should feel so strongly about it just then. She supposed it was pure anguish and frustration that made her whirl to him and say from the depths of her heart, 'I wish there was something I could do, Trent.'

He eyed her lingeringly where they stood in the shadows and remarked slowly, 'You're a strange girl, as I've said before.'

'Why?' she flashed a tear-bright gaze at him. 'Because I don't want Robert to die?'

'No. That's natural.' He shrugged this off, a mask over his own feelings and continued with a watchful smile, 'Half the time you fuss around Rob like an affectionate younger sister, but looking like you do now I could almost believe that he means everything to you.'

She lowered her gaze swiftly, deciding it was better to make no comment on this. Partly because she was emotionally cut-up and partly because she wanted to change the subject she said with a gesture of helplessness, 'Talking is so ineffective. If only there was something we could do! Robert is a sweet and sensitive person. He doesn't deserve to have his life cut short like this.'

Trent said with a grim look, 'It's a good job he's not here now to hear you talking like this.'

'Oh, it's all right for you men,' she flung at him impatiently, 'keeping everything bottled up inside. We're not like that. Sometimes it helps to have a good feminine bawl.'

'You can cry if you want to, but it won't cure Rob.' Trent spoke with steely self-control and Vivienne hated herself then. Knowing that he felt more deeply than she ever could, she slumped against him and cried into his chest, 'Oh, Trent! I do so want everything to go on being so wonderful for Robert. It's all been like some fabulous dream since we came to Tahad Island. I can't bear to think of anything spoiling it. I want it to go on and on.'

'Maybe it will,' Trent said gently. 'Maybe it will.' He stroked her hair, then looked down at her with his old grin. 'You wanted to try taking the boat to the cypress lagoon on the west side.'

She looked up expectantly. 'Can we?'

He nodded. 'I've made enquiries, and it's quite safe. According to the speed launch skipper there's mackerel and red snapper, bream and jew-fish there. But we'll have to be up at first light to appreciate the peace of the place.' He propelled her purposefully indoors and as she left him to go to her room she said with a sleepy smile, 'Robert will be thrilled.'

Though the days drifted pleasantly by both she and Trent knew it couldn't last. But what happened to bring an abrupt end to the idyllic island life was something neither of them had expected.

It was one afternoon when she had gone to the wood round the curve of the beach with Robert to see what birds they could find. They had spotted partridges and snipe and several colourful birds they didn't know the names of, and altogether the excursion had been highly successful. When they grew tired of looking at nature they turned their gazes towards the sea and sat and listened to the restful sound of the waves lapping over the rocks.

The path led straight up a gradual incline from the beach and Vivienne had often pushed Robert's wheelchair this far without any trouble. She usually perched on a rock somewhere near him and this afternoon she had chosen a smooth jutting section just below his footrest. Robert was in a mellow mood as he often was these days, being so close to nature. 'You know,' he said, his crinkled blue gaze trained towards the far horizon, 'I never thought I'd see so much sea. Living with it on your doorstep like this, and having it all around you, makes you realise what tiny beings we are.'

'It does have a sort of whittling down effect,' Vivienne agreed. She added laughingly, 'Now you know what it feels like living on a speck in the ocean.'

He nodded, taking in the views around him, then he said feelingly, 'You found me an island, Viv. I'll always be grateful to you for that.'

Always. How long was that in Robert's reckoning? A week? Two weeks? Steeling herself not to show any brightness in her eyes, she said gaily, 'I mustn't take all the credit. Trent was the one who badgered the owner to let us have this place.'

Robert smiled. He said thoughtfully, 'You two get along better these days.'

'Trent and I have always been friends,' she lied. And with lighthearted flattery, 'Who couldn't get along with a brother of yours?'

'You're easy to like yourself.' His gaze turned molten as he looked at her. 'You know I couldn't get along without you, Viv.'

Afraid that he was going to become over-emotional she said flippantly, 'Well, for the next half hour or so, you're going to have to try. Maurice has promised to show me the secret of his apple soufflé. And incidentally,' she looked at the sun lowering towards the sea, 'we ought to be getting back. We won't be able to take the short cut through the trees to the house if it gets too gloomy.'

'I suppose you're right.' He sighed, humorously resigned.

They were preparing to move off, and disaster in that peaceful spot was the furthest thing from their minds. Vivienne started to get lazily to her feet, then everything seemed to happen at once. She hadn't realised that the smoothness of the rock she had been sitting on would offer so dangerous a foothold. Not until the underside of her sandal came into contact, then it was too late. Skidding giddily, she could find no way of saving herself. She thought that Robert thrust a hand out to steady her, or she grabbed at the arm of his chair. Whatever, the next thing she knew was that she was splayed out where she had slipped and the wheelchair with Robert in it had gone hurtling down on to the rocks below.

It was only a drop of three or four feet and there were sand pockets out of reach of the sea. But when Vivienne picked herself up and saw the empty wheelchair and Robert crumpled on the rocks she almost fainted with fright. Her screams brought Trent and Haroun and the whole household.

By this time Robert had managed to pull himself into a sitting position. He saw the faces of those above him and said with a grin, 'Don't look so worried, everybody. I'm all right.' But his arm was twisted in a strange way and his face was ashen.

Trent had a doctor brought out from the mainland and for a while there was much commotion around the house. It was dark before things finally quietened down and Trent went to the boat to see the doctor off. Vivienne was waiting near the doorway when he returned, where they often stood to watch the moon playing on the sea through the pines. She turned dejectedly at the sound of his footsteps and asked in dull tones, 'How is he?'

'Better than we expected.' Trent spoke cheerfully, though she suspected this was mainly for her benefit. 'Rob's broken his wrist and picked up a few bruises. He's been given a sedative. He'll sleep till morning.'

'It was my fault, you know.' Vivienne flashed a tear-bright gaze at him.

Trent looked weary, but he spoke gently. 'Rob told me what happened. You slipped and he tried to save you. You don't have to blame yourself.'

'But I do!' The tears were more in evidence as she paced. 'I stupidly picked an unsafe place to sit and I hadn't the sense to see that the wheelchair was too close to the edge. And Robert——' she whirled on Trent. 'All he's had to go through and he had to go crashing down helplessly on to the rocks.' She wrung her hands and cried to the stars, 'Why couldn't it have been me!'

'You would have come off a lot worse,' Trent said in clipped tones. 'Rob was a rugby player, remember. He knew how to fall.' He reached an arm out to steady her, his voice considerably softer. 'Take a hold on yourself, Vivienne. Accidents happen.'

'But we'll have to go back?' Her eyes searched his face questioningly.

'I'm afraid so,' Trent nodded. 'Rob will have to have his wrist set, and in his condition it wouldn't be wise for him to remain on the island. But there's no reason why life should be any less attractive at the villa ... is there?' He was watching her closely.

'No ... of course not.' She tried to sound cheerfully re-signed. She led the way indoors to start packing, a pulse hammering in her throat. They were going back to Koudia and she couldn't tell Trent why she was afraid.

CHAPTER EIGHT

ROBERT suffered considerable pain with his wrist and for a day or two after their return to Koudia he was compelled to take things quietly. The fall had shaken him more than he cared to admit and though his grin was very much in evidence he looked weak and ill from the shock. Vivienne read to him, mainly poetry from his favourite volumes, in the shade of the trees near the pool. She wished she could have pleased him more by speaking the words as he liked to hear them. Sometimes he read to her to give her some idea how a poem should go, and she was inwardly moved then by the depth of feeling in his voice.

He retired to his rooms early in the afternoons and she was left with long hours to fill in the evenings, once Trent had left for the casino. She spent the time browsing round the books in the library and even playing an occasional record in modulated tones. She had developed a strong reluctance to going to her room until the last possible moment before bed. One night she had gone up rather late and was on the point of running a tepid bath before slipping between the sheets when the sight of a shadowy figure out on the balcony brought her heart into her throat. Gary drifted up to the open doorway and looked around the luxuriously furnished room with a surly smile on his lips.

'You do all right for yourself, don't you, playing sweethearts with the brother of a rich casino owner.'

Vivienne hurried across to the door with a chalk-white face and gasped, 'Gary! You shouldn't have come!' She looked around wildly and took him by the arm. 'We can't talk here.'

'Oh, I don't know.' He lingered mulishly, his glance taking in the tastefully lit interior, the damask-draped bed. 'It looks the ideal place for a chat to me. Cosy ... comfortable ...'

'The *minzah*,' Vivienne was tugging him cajolingly. 'You know we'll be much safer there.'

As though he knew she was talking sense he moved at last with her down the steps, but in such a stubborn, oddly smiling way that her nerves screamed at the risk they were taking. It seemed an age before they were stumbling into the doorway of the *minzah*, Vivienne having half tugged, half pulled him along the route through the mimosa thicket. She thought her heart would burst from the effort and the choking anxiety, but Gary had no intention of giving her breathing space. He pulled her to him as soon as they were in the ruined pavilion and said with a sulky gleam, 'You didn't tell me you were going away. I suppose you thought it was one big joke, me coming up here and finding the place all closed up?'

'There wasn't time.' Vivienne winced a little at his roughness. 'It was all decided on the spur of the moment. I couldn't possibly have got word to you.'

His smile sloped cruelly for a moment, then his grip on her eased and he spoke in more agreeable tones. 'Well, it was damned inconvenient you disappearing like that, but you're back now, so what does it matter?' He put his arms about her and let his mouth travel over her throat, asking, 'Did you miss me?'

'Well ... I didn't have time to think much.' Forcing a smile, she drew away from him slightly. 'Things were rather hectic, and Robert had an accident. That's why we had to come home.'

'What kind of an accident? He's all right, isn't he?'

She thought there was a sharpness in Gary's tones.

'He broke his wrist,' she explained. 'He was shaken up, that's all, but it didn't help his condition.'

'No, well, it wouldn't, would it?' Gary said almost jokingly. His embrace tightened and he added thickly, 'Anyway, that's enough talk about junior for the time being. You and I have got quite a bit of ground to make up.' He planted his mouth on hers and explored her lips with a kind of brutal satisfaction, then lifting his head briefly he muttered, 'I can't think why you dragged us away from your room. We could have made a night of it there with the curtains drawn.'

Vivienne found herself straining away from him and saying rather shakily, 'Really, Gary! I don't know how you can suggest such a thing, knowing there's a young invalid in the house.'

'You always were a bit of a prude, if I remember rightly,' he smiled sensuously. 'But you're older now, and older girls change.'

His hands were clumsily roaming her body and with a feeling of revulsion she pushed him away and snapped, 'I haven't changed *that* much!' Some distance apart from him in the darkness she told him quiveringly, 'I don't know what you expected coming here at this hour of the night, but if it's what I think, then the sooner you leave, the better!'

She saw the glint of Gary's eyes in the gloom. That smile, a little vicious now, was still on his lips. 'Our eager little Vivienne has cooled all of a sudden, hasn't she?' he murmured. 'You searched me out, remember? Turned the city upside down, so you told me. You were all over me with your sob story of the kid in the wheelchair, now it seems you'd prefer to forget our little meetings and the fact that you and I were once—shall we say—romantically attached. I wonder why?'

This was something that Vivienne had asked herself often during the past days, but this was no time for self-analysis.

'You can talk!' she retorted smoothly. 'That night when I first saw you at the chemin-de-fer table in the casino, you weren't in too big a hurry to drag yourself away from the game, as I remember it.'

'Of course not, my sweet. You don't think *you* were the main attraction for all this cloak and dagger stuff? Do you imagine I've been taking care to mix openly with Colby's friends at the casino and biding my time as a forgotten Romeo because of fond memories of *you*?'

'I think you'd better explain what you mean by that.' Vivienne spoke calmly, though a horrible fear was beginning to make itself felt in the pit of her stomach.

'Gladly.' Gary's face and eyes hardened around his smile. 'I lack the means to live on a grand scale. There are hundreds like me in Tangier. We rub along, scraping a living where we can, waiting for that one-off chance that will bring in the big money. Well, I've found mine.'

Vivienne's voice was faint, but she managed to say clearly, 'I don't understand any of this talk, Gary. And I'd rather not hear any more. Perhaps you should go now.'

'All right,' he shrugged, and moved towards the opening. 'But I can't promise that your precious Robert won't have his dreams disturbed.'

Vivienne felt a stab of apprehension. She asked swiftly, 'What has Robert got to do with it?'

'Everything, darling.' Gary turned, sure of himself, and faced her. 'That's why you'd better not be in too big a hurry to get rid of me. You see, my sweet, I've got a plan. And my plan is this. Colby has pots of money; I haven't a bean. He wouldn't like his invalid brother to know what's going on, so in exchange we're going to relieve him of a little of that disgusting wealth.'

Vivienne's blood froze. She said in a shaky voice, 'What makes you think I'd be a party to anything dishonest?'

'The fact that I'm prepared to go to Robert and explain the whole story of you standing in for this Lucy what's-her-name,' Gary said blithely.

Vivienne swayed. She reached out for support and gasped, 'You couldn't! It would kill him!'

'I know, my love. That's why I think you're going to do as I say. Now listen.' Gary's tones became harsh and businesslike. 'I've wasted enough time waiting for you to show up, and I'm not prepared to put this thing off any longer. Here's what you do. You're well known at the casino and you know Trent's habits. I've watched him myself and

discovered that he leaves his office round about midnight
and spends much of the time after that in the gaming
rooms. Right. Tomorrow night you and I are going to find
some excuse to go to his office *after* midnight. We shouldn't
be disturbed while we're cleaning him out of the casino
takings.'

Vivienne stared, horrified. 'You're mad if you think you
can get away with anything like that,' she gasped. 'The
money's in a safe and only Trent has the key. Also he
always locks the office door when he goes into the gaming
rooms.'

'Well, that will be up to you, darling,' Gary said
breezily. 'Likely as not there'll be two sets of keys—he'll
have to relegate responsibility some time. And living in the
same house you'll know where his rooms are. I'm sure
you'll manage somehow!'

Vivienne blanched in the darkness. 'Do you actually
think I would go searching for safe keys in Trent's room?'
she asked quiveringly.

'I don't think, I *know*, poppet,' Gary said with a thin
smile. 'You're too fond of Robert to see him get hurt. Now
don't let's waste any more time. I've got to be going, and
you ought to get back to your room in case you're missed.
I'll see you tomorrow night at the casino at about eleven-
thirty. And if you're entertaining any ideas of not turning
up, forget it. It will be the worse for the wheelchair kid if
you do.'

Vivienne stood riveted in the darkness. He turned in the
opening and she could see his smile faintly as he touched
his brow in mock salute. 'So long, Viv, my sweet. Pleasant
dreams.' Then he was gone.

How she got back to her room she never remembered.
Sick with fear and disgust, she clung to the bed drapes, the
lights spinning as she tried to think clearly. Wasn't it all
some horrible nightmare? Wouldn't she wake in a moment
and find herself breathing a sigh of relief? If only she
could!

She clutched limply for a chair unable to believe what

had just happened. Gary, the man she had once thought she was in love with—oh yes, she knew that now—cheerfully stooping to this level! Right back to that first meeting at the casino she hadn't wanted to admit it to herself, but she knew he had changed. Always a little rakish, he had become more dissipated than ever, yet she had foolishly clung to a dream; the dream of herself as she had been at nineteen, believing what she had felt then had been love.

While other teenage girls passed painlessly through the growing pains of romance, she had held fast stubbornly, because her pride had been hurt no doubt, to something that had been no more than a holiday infatuation. How clearly she saw it all now. Or to come nearer the truth, hadn't she known it from that first moment in the casino gardens when Gary had taken her in his arms?

She shook herself, a wave of panic seizing her, and moved agitatedly about the room. What good would it do going into all that now? She had become hopelessly entangled with Gary. She had trusted him by telling him of the role she was playing at Koudia. Now he threatened to go to Robert with the truth. *Would he do it?* She pressed her hands to her mouth in an agony of picturing the scene. He would. She knew him to have a ruthless streak. She thought of Robert. He loved her, believing her to be Lucy, the writer of all those letters. How would he stand up now to being told that she, Vivienne, was an impostor; someone who had agreed to stand in to keep him happy because Lucy considered herself too plain? He wouldn't. It would break him in every way. Her face was a ghastly white as she sat down icily calm now. Whatever else Robert must never know.

After a sleepless night she rose and dressed shakily and went down to breakfast. Luckily it was Robert's day for the hospital, so she had only to get through the meal with a bright smile pasted on her lips. She managed because she told herself that Gary's plan to ransack the casino safe seemed hopelessly bizarre and fantastic by the light of day.

But later on when she was drifting towards the pool, the full force of what he expected her to do hit her in such a way that she almost sank to her knees before she reached her chair. Trent, making for the table with his briefcase under his arm, gripped her as she stumbled and demanded, his probing gaze raking her drained features, 'What's wrong? You didn't have two words to say at the breakfast table.'

'A touch of the sun, I suppose.' She tried to sound cheerful, but her voice came out horribly cracked and shaky. 'I'll just lie down for a while. I'm sure it will pass.'

Trent pulled a lounger into the shade of the sun umbrella and she sank down feeling so sick with nerves it was something of a shock to look up and see his blue eyes and to hear him ask, 'That better?'

Vivienne nodded, unable to speak, but in that moment she would have given anything for the comfort of his touch. *His touch.* She thought of that night in his office at the casino when he had crouched to rub balm over the bruise on her shin, and of the time on Tahad island when he had smoothed her hair against his chest. And there was comfort just in remembering. She couldn't recall a time when she hadn't known a kind of vague contentment at Trent's nearness. She had wanted it to go on. She had even devised the plan of an enforced holiday to cheat a little. It was only now when that contentment was threatened, when something too awful to think about was going to shatter it completely, that the truth dawned. As the mists of her past and her entanglement with Gary receded, blown away for ever by the overwhelming clarity of this new emotion, the hidden rapture came to light and she knew that no man would ever mean as much to her as Trent did. What she had felt for Gary seemed puny indeed compared to the overwhelming force of her love for the man beside her; like a flickering spark against a strong and everlasting flame.

All this came to her in a flash as often infinite wisdom will, and she realised that her gaze was still locked with Trent's above her. From where her head lay on the flowered cushion she was stricken with an urge to tell him the whole crazy story. And as he looked down at her she felt that he was waiting in some way for whatever she had to say. She clung for a moment to what was offered there, then her lashes flickered down and she said, putting on a careless air, 'Don't let me upset things. I'll just keep quiet here in the shade.'

Inwardly wretched, she knew she had no choice but to do as Gary said. Trent wouldn't miss the money in his safe and Lucy's secret would remain intact.

From beneath her lowered lashes she sensed that Trent had moved away and taken his chair at the table. She lay sinkingly, her mind in a turmoil. Fortunately Robert was safe at the hospital. But the thought of having to lay her hands on the key to the safe before tonight put her in a cold sweat.

By lunch time she felt limp with anxiety and nerves, yet she dare not let Trent think that she was ill. She went through the courses at the table with him making the usual small talk, hardly knowing what she ate as her mind wrestled with the problem of the key. Somehow she had to find a way of making a search of Trent's room when he was otherwise occupied. But how? How?

She couldn't still the trembling of her hands and occasionally she was clumsy with her knife and fork. At one time she almost knocked over her water glass.

Trent, watching her, remarked tersely, 'It might be a good idea to rest in your room this afternoon, with the blinds drawn. It looks like more than a touch of sun to me.'

'I'm perfectly all right now.' Vivienne's glance flew to his. She had to get to the casino tonight.

'Just the same, you'd better do as I say,' he replied firmly.

She didn't want to cross him in any way, so going all out to appear agreeable she said lightly, 'I did have a bit of a head this morning. I suppose an hour or two would sort of ... refresh me for the evening.' It didn't help to find herself swaying as she stood up after the meal. Trent offered her a steadying hand and escorted her to the door. It was then that a heaven-sent opportunity dropped into her lap.

The Berber foreman who managed the fruit orchards was waiting outside in the hall. He usually came to the house to report about once a week and this involved a long session with Trent in the library going through the accounts. This would give her time to search for the keys she had to find. Abdul had gone to eat in the servants' quarters. She would have the house to herself.

Faint with apprehension at what she was about to attempt, she fought back the nausea and made her way across the hall. She felt that Trent's glance followed her thoughtfully as she went up the stairs. She stayed in her room only a few minutes, then quietly went out of the door again. Along one of the corridors upstairs she could get into the left wing, where Trent had his rooms on the floor below Robert's.

It took her several minutes to find her way, but she knew that door facing the left wing staircase. She had passed it often when going up to Robert's rooms, and occasionally she had seen Abdul leaving with items of clothing of Trent's over his arm, destined for the cleaners. Swiftly she turned the knob and slipped inside.

She didn't allow herself the luxury of lingering in a room so personal to Trent, though she was tempted to run her fingers lovingly over an odd tie thrown over a chair; over the books on a low wall shelf beside the bed. If fright hadn't been dogging at her heels she would have seen far more to interest her in Trent's apartment; as it was most of it reeled before her eyes as she tried to think, think!

Undoubtedly he would be carrying the keys of the casino on his person, but it was fairly certain that there would be a spare set. The problem was where to look. Vivienne fumbled, panic in her throat, among the pockets of his suits in the wall wardrobe, flicked through a chest of drawers which contained his shirts; tried the bedside locker, and the drawer of a rather beautiful carved table near the window. Then the idea hit her: the desk which she could just see in the other room. She stumbled through and across the carpet towards it, praying that the drawers would not be locked. She was careful not to disturb the papers there. Every drawer contained nothing but papers, papers. And then in a tiny drawer to the left she experienced the horrible flush of success. There, nestling beside a business diary and an Arab dictionary, was a key ring holding three or four small keys.

They felt icy cold in her grasp, though it was a hot afternoon. She felt the same kind of cold feathering the back of her neck and the dew on her temples as she stole back towards the door. A last look round to see that she had disturbed nothing and then she was outside.

Barely had she turned from the door than her heart flew into her mouth, for there, coming up round the curve of the staircase, was Trent. Every vestige of colour drained from her face as she asked herself frantically, had he seen her coming out of his room? Or had she been just a second ahead of him? There was nothing she could do but hope for the best. She thought he was eyeing her rather sharply and to smooth over a horrible moment she said glibly, 'I've just been up to Robert's room to see if I could find his bird book. There's a lovely green bird in the tree outside my room and I wanted to find out its name.'

'A bee-eater, probably,' Trent said. And still eyeing her he added, 'I thought you were going to have a lie down.'

'I was actually ... but this bird ...' she finished lamely, her voice giving way. She wished in that moment that she could be spirited to the other side of the world. But magically the danger passed and Trent was saying, 'I told you to draw the blinds. You won't get any rest staring at the outside glare. Try it. It's good for the nerves.'

Had he noticed that she was shaking like a leaf? Perhaps not. 'Yes, Trent.' Meekly she turned and went back in the direction of her own room.

Once inside she collapsed on the bed, the keys biting into the palm of her hand where she had gripped them. *Never*,

never would she want to go through that again. As it turned out, she did spend the whole afternoon lying down. There was no question of her legs supporting her for some time after *that* ordeal. Nor had she any strength to face the evening to come. But face it she must.

She didn't go downstairs until it was time for dinner. She was terrified that Trent would notice her ghostly paleness. He told her over the meal that his brother had come home weary from the hospital and gone straight to bed. This at least was a crumb of comfort to her, just knowing that Robert was safe in his room.

She wanted to give the impression of having a healthy appetite and ate though the food choked her. And blithely, though a little shakily, she said when they were approaching the coffee stage, 'I think I'll drop in at the casino this evening. I feel like a change of air.'

Trent, whose glance had never been far from her since she had joined him at the table, commented on a harsh note, 'I'd forget that if I were you. You don't look capable of making two steps beyond the outside door.'

'Oh, but I am!' Her pleading gaze lifted swiftly to his and it was all she could do to keep the tears of stress from brimming there.

She heard his heavy exhalation of breath. His expression was speculative again, although he conceded easily enough, 'Okay, if that's what you want. I'll tell Abdul that he's to drive you down at whatever time you like.'

Relief flooded over her that he hadn't offered to take her with him himself, but she tried to sound offhand. 'Oh, it will probably be only for an hour, later on. Just for something to do.'

She didn't linger once the meal was over. She mumbled some excuse about having things to do in her room and left Trent to smoke his cigarette on his own.

It seemed an age before she heard his car leave for the casino. She waited, pacing, her heartbeats counting the seconds, until at last it was eleven and time to go downstairs. Abdul was on hand and somehow Vivienne made it to the car, though her knees were shaking badly.

She had put on a silk dress suitable for evening and though the night air was warm she shivered with the cold prickle of fear as the car made its way through the town. The head and shoulders of the reliable and faithful Abdul beyond the glass partition heartened her, and at one point she was crazily tempted to ask him to take her somewhere, anywhere other than the casino. Despite his Arab hauteur he had a gentle streak where she was concerned and she knew he would have driven her to wherever she had a mind to go. But that wouldn't stop Gary. She knew all too well that he had familiarised himself with the grounds of Koudia and the house, for just such a night as this, and would even find his way up to Robert's room, if pushed. So she sat limp on her seat and allowed herself to be driven to the casino.

The sea front was rowdy and, no doubt obeying Trent's orders Abdul remained close at her side until they had entered the Café Anglais. It was scant comfort to find that the place was crowded. If the position had been reversed perhaps Gary wouldn't have had the nerve to carry out his reckless plan. Abdul left Vivienne with his salaam and she wandered between the tables hardly aware of the din because her head was pounding with another kind of distraction. When a hand fastened tightly around her wrist she knew it was Gary.

'Hi!' He put on a look with which one might greet an old friend and said between his lips that were thinly smiling, 'Shall we find a table?'

Vivienne went with him slackly and they sat down at a spot not far from the bar. As soon as he had got the business of ordering the drinks over with, Gary said beneath his breath and his smile, 'I'm glad to see you using your head, my sweet. I take it you've got the keys?'

Vivienne reached for her handbag. She started to open it, then closed it again and blurted, 'Gary, please tell me this is all some horrible joke.' She looked at him beseechingly. 'If you burst out laughing right now I won't mind.

I'll be only too happy to join in, if you'll only tell me that
that's all it is—a joke.'

'Of course it's a joke, darling. And it will be on Colby
when we've cleaned out his safe. Now give me the keys,' he
demanded, deadly serious behind his smile, 'and do as I
say. In a few minutes we're going to take a little stroll
through into the gaming rooms, just to let it be known that
I'm a good friend of yours and Colby's, so to speak. We'll
do one or two little excursions through the vestibule where
the casino attendants keep a watch, for the same purpose.
When Colby leaves his office at midnight to circulate
among his guests in the gaming rooms, we'll make our way
there as though expecting to join him in a late night drink.'

To Vivienne the next half hour was a succession of tor-
tuous moments in a pandemonium world where everyone
seemed to laugh too much, to talk too much, where the hum
of the gaming rooms made her head feel as though it was
bursting as she moved in a kind of numb stupor doing all
the things that Gary told her to do.

There was only one moment when she saw things with
sufficient clarity to feel the lead weight of her emotions inside. That was a little after twelve when she saw Trent
talking with a group of friends beside the casino bar. The
women brushing close to him were the svelte types in clinging evening gowns and she remembered dimly her joke,
*Every Eden has its serpent complete with innumerable
Eves*. That was in the days when she had wanted something to carp about where Trent was concerned, perhaps
because even then her subconscious had felt the need to
fight off the effect of his insidious charm. Well, it hadn't
done her any good. She had discovered that he had chosen
to run a casino not for any ulterior gain, but purely as a
business pastime for the evenings. But she would have
loved him anyway. She knew that now. As she craved for
something in return. Just a smile, as he was smiling now at
his beautiful companions; the touch of his arm across her
shoulders as she had known it on other evenings. But all she
could do was watch the svelte females competing for his at-

tention when she ached to be the one closest to him.

She felt Gary's grip on her wrist telling her that the moment she had been dreading was close at hand. 'Now's our chance,' he said in her ear. 'The big boss has got himself nicely encumbered. The job should go like a dream.'

But they still had to get into the office. Vivienne thought that Gary was being naïvely optimistic about this part of his plan, yet when they strolled through the vestibule a second or two later and along towards the office door no one interfered with them.

Gary took a chance furtively with one of the keys, found it didn't fit, and tried another while Vivienne felt the hairs rising on the back of her neck, sure that they were being observed. Then the door was open and Gary was firmly propelling her inside. He shut the door quickly and locked it, commenting with a low chuckle, 'What did I tell you? Nothing to it!'

He seemed to have a good idea where the safe was and while Vivienne stood paralysed beside the desk she watched him experiment again with the bunch of keys. In a few seconds before her horrified gaze, the door of the safe swung open. It needed only a glance to see that it was filled with banknotes in various currencies, thick wads of them in neat piles. As though mesmerised she followed Gary's movements. He had brought out a square pack from his pocket which when unfolded became a roomy yet compact holdall, and this he proceeded to fill with the money from the safe.

If Vivienne had wanted to talk some sense into him, even at this late stage it would have been useless, for no sound would come from her fear-racked throat. Nevertheless she was endeavouring to croak out something when all her nerves screamed to attention, for there at the door was the sound of *another* key turning in the lock. While she was grasping at the desk for support, the door opened and Trent stepped in.

'Good evening, Vivienne.' His face showed no surprise at what he saw. He was even a little laconic. 'Aren't you going to introduce me to your friend? The one you got to know in Tangier four years ago, isn't it?'

He locked the door soundlessly behind him, and Vivienne wished quietly that she could die. Gary on the other hand swaggered and it was obvious that he had decided to try and brazen it out. 'That's right,' though considerably paler, he replied jauntily. 'Viv and I have been close for a long time. Too bad she didn't tell you about our little romance.'

'It is unfortunate, but not altogether unexpected,' Trent commented with steely calm. 'However, we won't go into that now. I'll take the keys, if you don't mind.'

As though he realised the futility of pitting himself against a man such as Trent, Gary threw the keys sulkily on to the desk. Trent retrieved them, then he took a few bills from one of the wads of banknotes. 'You've got an hour to leave the country. There's a plane flying out at twelve forty-five.' He tossed the fare on to the desk. 'And if I were you, I wouldn't come back. You might find the authorities hot on your trail.'

Gary opened his mouth as though about to attempt more bravado, thought better of it and picked up the money. With indomitable cool Trent went ahead of him to unlock the door. As he passed Vivienne Gary threw her a sickly smile, then he went out and the door closed behind him.

Vivienne, still clutching the desk, was all too aware of the crushing silence with only herself and Trent in the room. She saw the pallor of his face now, the way the skin was stretched taut over his cheekbones and around his dilated nostrils as he struggled with something which she could only put down to anger. He approached her, his eyes glinting with steely contempt, then distaste in his tones he spoke at last. 'Robert believes in you and to me that's all that counts. As I said on the day of your arrival, you'll go through with what you started and like it.' He picked up the phone on the desk and said a few staccato words into it. Almost at once the door opened and she was dismissed with an icy, 'Abdul will take you home.'

Hardly trusting her legs, she moved towards the door and the imperturbable face of the manservant. *They had known. They had all known, or at least suspected.* She felt it now. Her clumsy attempts at the house to steal the keys had not gone unnoticed. Trent had seen to it that she was not molested in any way after her arrival at the casino, though all the time he had been watching her closely. With perfect timing he had returned to his office and caught Gary before the open safe.

White as a ghost, she went out with Abdul and through the noisy café to the car. The gay, late night activity and summer revelry, the laughing faces of the people in the streets, seemed to mock at her raw and prostrate senses as the car took her back to Koudia.

Upstairs in her room she fell exhausted into bed, but the soothing veil of sleep was not to be hers. Through the long dark hours all she could see in her mind was Trent's face, taut with anger and distaste. The only sound in her ears, his voice, biting in its contempt.

CHAPTER NINE

ROBERT was not to be seen at the poolside on the brilliant afternoons when insects murmured lazily in the heat and the flower of the hibiscus glowed blood red in the shade. He had shown no signs of recovering from his last exhausting trip to the hospital and spent the best part of his day in bed. Vivienne sat with him for a few hours each afternoon carefully hiding her fright at his listlessness and sunken features. Though he smiled and joked with her and played cards with considerable zest despite his plastered wrist, he dozed a lot of the time and she was left holding his hand and gazing with a choked-up feeling at his racked boyish face. Her own heartache seemed nothing when she considered what he was having to smile through.

Trent had not spoken again of that fateful night when he had surprised her and Gary in his office. On the occasions when they spent the time together with Robert he was agreeable and courteous. In the evenings they went through the ritual of dining together in the room overlooking the Casbah. Momeen, always effusive and eager to project a feeling of cheer in the sick household, looked from one to the other of them anxiously as he served the meal. But Trent's conversation was always pleasant, his manners impeccable. Yet Vivienne knew, miserably, that he despised her.

He didn't go to the casino in the evenings now. Since Robert's condition had deteriorated he had left it to Abdul to run things at the Café Anglais, with, no doubt Marcel the head croupier assisting. Vivienne knew that Trent paced the downstairs rooms at night, and that sometimes he walked alone in the grounds. She knew because she spent the nights in much the same way, and because every part of her was aware of him.

It seemed to her so cruelly unjust that he should think what he did of her. It was obvious he believed that she was in love with Gary, that she had schemed out the whole thing with him over these past weeks and, regardless of Robert, had planned to abscond with Gary and the money that same evening. That was what Trent believed and that was what drove her to pace at nights with the bright tears of hurt in her eyes. Until the moment came when she could endure the misery of such thoughts no longer. If she had been the heroine in a book she would have gone on stoic-ally playing her part, protecting those she had sworn to protect. But she wasn't a heroine, she was human flesh and blood, and she couldn't go on, knowing that Trent thought that of her. *Not even for Lucy.* She was Vivienne Blyth and she wanted to think, feel and *love* as Vivienne Blyth.

The tears were hot on her eyelids that particular night as she went along the balcony outside her room and down the side steps to the terrace below. There had been a heavy summer shower earlier on in the day and the wet earth was pungent with herb-like fragrances and the cloying sweet-ness of wet blossom. She knew that Trent was out there in the grounds and heedless of the damp and her thin dress she picked her way along the shrouded poolside and through the hibiscus hedge opening. A segment of moon in a rainwashed sky cast a pewter polish over the sea, remind-ing her achingly of those nights on Tahad island.

She saw Trent on the path beside the Moorish arbour. His face, as she approached, was paled by the moon's rays and chiselled out against the night. She moved in, knowing that he was aware of her, for he spoke harshly. 'You shouldn't be out here. There's a chill in the air.'

'I'm all right,' impatiently she shook off his concern and moving restlessly, wondered where she should start. With Trent preoccupied and grimly withdrawn it wasn't easy. Plunging in, she said, her voice wavering, 'Will you believe me when I tell you that Robert means almost as much to me as he does to you?'

'Sure! I'll believe anything you say,' Trent shrugged with a bitingly ironic smile.

Vivienne closed her eyes momentarily, then continued quiveringly, 'I suppose I'd better start at the beginning. You were right about me—I'm not the genuine product.' She tilted her chin at him. 'You've never heard of a girl called Lucy Miles, but she is the one, not me, who wrote all those letters to Robert.' Seeing Trent's mild change of expression, she went on with a cracked laugh of despair, 'Don't ask me why! Lucy's a sweet and gentle person, but she got this silly notion that she was too plain and simple for Robert's tastes, so she sent him a photograph of me.'

Trent's gaze narrowed and he said beneath his breath, 'That was an idiotic thing to do.'

'Agreed,' Vivienne replied abruptly. 'The idea was that she was going to confess at some later date when her relationship with Robert was solid enough to stand the jolt. Then you wrote and told her that Robert wouldn't get well and she went completely to pieces.'

Trent's eyes had become slightly glittery as he looked at her. 'How was it you came in her place?' he rasped.

'She asked me to. I didn't want to, but I could see her point about it being a horrible shock for Robert in his condition to be confronted by someone he would take for a complete stranger.'

There was a deathly silence and then, 'She started the myth by sending your photograph and asked you to keep it up until Robert ...' Trent rocked back on his heels, his breath hissing through clenced teeth, 'Of all the crazy, harebrained schemes!'

'If you knew Lucy you wouldn't say that,' Vivienne spoke up loyally. 'She was thinking of Robert. That's why she persuaded me to come, to save him any last-minute disappointment.' Her voice softened considerably. 'You have to remember that Lucy loves Robert deeply, and people in love do some odd things.'

'Are you speaking from experience?' Trent asked with a sneer.

'I suppose, by that, you mean Gary Thornton?' Vivienne said quietly. She became restless again and spoke on the move. 'I did think I was in love with him once. I even went to a great deal of trouble to look him up when I found myself back in Tangier, as you probably guessed.'

'I had an idea that something was going on. I decided to give you enough rope in the hope that you'd trip yourself up. And you did!' Trent nodded grimly. 'Go on.'

Vivienne did as he asked deflatedly. 'It turned out that Gary's favourite haunt was the casino. I met him there that first evening I went. I soon discovered that I too had been chasing a myth; that Gary meant nothing at all to me. But not before I'd foolishly told him about Lucy and me.'

While she had been speaking she thought she saw something leap in Trent's eyes, something that was just as swiftly doused again. She became still and he said deeply, 'You were afraid of something. I gathered that.'

'I suppose I was,' she smiled a little distractedly. 'I wanted to get away, and we went to Tahad island. But Gary was waiting for me when I got back. He threatened to tell Robert the whole story of the fake role I was playing unless I got him the keys to your safe.' She looked at Trent then. 'What could I do?'

'You could have told me,' he rapped.

'I thought about it.' For a long moment her gaze clung to his. 'But there was Lucy to consider. And I was terrified that Gary might still find a way to get to Robert.'

'You little idiot!' Trent took her by the shoulders. 'You went through that alone. The fellow could have done you real harm.'

'But he didn't,' she shrugged. 'He got nothing at all for his trouble except what he deserved. And ... well, now you know.'

'That's right. Now I know.' She felt his fingers roughly caressing her shoulders. His face in the shadows had a look that held her spellbound, and nothing seemed more natural to her, after the weeks of being close to one another in so many different ways, than to be here with Trent now like this. His eyes on her glowed in a peculiar way, then she was in his arms.

His lips on hers opened up the floodgates of her emotions so that she melted weakly against him. And Trent too was like a man possessed as he rained kisses on her face and throat; by what? she wondered ecstatically. Could it be that Trent felt as deeply for her as she did for him? There was something in the savage way he claimed her with his lips, in the hungry caressing of his hands through her thin dress. Then while she was drowning in the aching sweetness of his nearness he put her abruptly away from him and shaking his head with his back to her he bit out hoarsely, 'Get the hell out of my sight!'

Vivienne ran most of the way back to the house, her eyes wet with tears and the despair in her worse than anything she had ever known. As far as Trent was concerned she belonged to Robert and nothing, nothing would ever change that!

There was another heavy shower the next day and then the storm blowing in from Spain rained itself out and the sun came out again in full glory to deepen the sea to a royal blue and to pick out the brilliant colours of the flowers and blossoms at Koudia. There was a sparkle about the days again, a clarity of vision when one looked at the hills and landscape around Tangier. But to Vivienne so much colour hurt the senses. It was almost as if the world was mocking with all it possessed at the desolate atmosphere at the villa; at the feeling of torment and hopelessness that was now an everyday part of living.

Robert seldom left his room and as he spent most of his day in bed he became more and more dependent on Vivienne's company. It wasn't difficult to put on a bright front, for he was always cheerful, but behind her smile her heart ached at the physical change in him. She and Trent spent long sessions with him keeping him amused. Neither she nor Trent had referred again to that evening beside the Moorish arbour, not by word of mouth or look, but sometimes their glances met and held for a second, then she would feel an agonising surge of tenderness inside.

Robert's moods gave no opportunity for gloom. One evening he managed to get to the table for dinner. Every known device was used to celebrate the occasion. The table gleamed with crystal-ware and silver. The candelabra added a soft glow and the jewelled lights of Tangier were spread out below the open windows. No one wanted to admit that there was a hollow ring about the happy atmosphere of the upstairs rooms. To Vivienne the occasion was all the more touching because Trent, showing his age but joking as always, appeared particularly endearing, and because he scrupulously avoided looking her way.

On the other evenings they dined together as always downstairs. Vivienne couldn't imagine doing otherwise, although the barrier that lay between them now was far more manifest than any that had existed between them in the past. They went through the courses that Momeen served, hands sometimes no more than a space away as something was reached for across the table, but a space that might as well have been a million miles in distance, so keenly felt was the barrier.

Afterwards, out on the little vine-covered terrace adjoining the room, they would go through the bitter-sweet ritual of smoking the one cigarette of the day. Where the scents of oleander and jasmine drifted in from the gardens Trent would reach into his pocket for his cigarette case and afterwards flick his lighter under hers and then his own, and his glance on her would look about to linger, then remain steady on the flame instead, and she would feel that she was coming close to losing her sanity. How could she bear it, loving Trent, knowing that he loved her, yet knowing no contact? Not so much as the touch of his hand on hers. If only they could have allowed themselves that!

One evening when she felt she would buckle under the tension, there was a slight commotion indoors. Haroun was standing in the doorway from the hall and Momeen was hovering over the silver dishes on the table looking slightly flustered. 'It is the young master,' he stammered when Trent went through. 'He is asking for some of Monsieur Maurice's date meringue.'

Vivienne felt her heart turn over. Was this to be one of Robert's last requests? Trent asked levelly, 'Is there any left?'

Momeen examined the dishes and nodded his head vigorously. 'There is indeed.'

'Well, if that's what he wants, have some sent up,' Trent said in the same level tones.

Her throat aching furiously, Vivienne hurried away to her room.

The following morning she swam languidly in the pool for an hour. She knew that Trent exercised in the water around dawn each day and she studiously avoided going down until he had returned to his rooms. There was no sign of life from the house as she kicked water listlessly between the floating armchairs.

In the afternoon, medical routine being what it was, a young Moorish doctor accompanied a portable X-ray unit which had been sent to give the latest results of Robert's wrist. It was a cumbersome business getting the contraption upstairs along with the three technicians needed, but with Abdul, slightly imperious when directing his own kind, the operation was carried out fairly smoothly. Vivienne, arranging flowers in one of the rooms looking on to the terrace, hadn't expected to hear any more for a while—not at least until the technicians made their way down again. But curiously enough, after some time had elapsed it was the doctor who appeared. He came down the stairs and rushed straight for the phone.

Looking through the doorway into the hall she couldn't make out his rapid speech, but he seemed oddly excited in some way. Trent was standing in the doorway of the library. She saw him walk across enquiringly to the Moorish doctor and after more rapid conversation they both went back into the library and closed the door. Vivienne's hands trembled as she tried to make something of the carnations and honeysuckle in the vase. What was wrong? Was it something terrible to do with Robert?

It seemed an age to her before the two men came out of the library again and made their way upstairs. She wandered about the room seeing nothing of the exquisite furnishing, the intricately patterned ceiling and delicate wall panels. Though she examined the elaborate designs on wallside bureaux and fingered the ornate handles of the drawers, she was really blind to all that she looked at, for her mind was straining in every possible way to that upstairs room in the house.

Then, when she was expecting to see some activity in the direction of the stairs, it was something of a surprise to find that it came at her back, through the windows which looked on to the front terrace. Beyond the line of shady archways a sombre-looking car had drawn up, and she recognised the man who was stepping out as one of the French specialists who attended Robert. He was a thick-set man with iron grey hair and ageing handsome features. Wearing light summer shirt and slacks and white tennis shoes, he went hurriedly indoors.

Abdul came to escort him upstairs and Vivienne was left with only stillness again. She could stand the indoors no longer and speedily made her way out to the flower gardens beyond the pool. She made a determined effort to gather some more exotic blooms to brighten the house, but it was only by gritting her teeth and holding on that she managed to control the urge to rush indoors and follow the others to Robert's room.

Her ears tuned that way, she heard voices eventually in the distance approaching the outdoors, and above the pounding of her pulses the departure of the specialist's car. As calmly as she could she walked back alongside the pool towards the house. The men with the X-ray unit were just leaving as she took the steps beside the low palms to the terrace. Trent, who had been seeing them off, turned and looked her way and she realised only then that her arms were laden with the blooms she had blindly picked without thinking in her anxiety.

He said, with a lazy smile, coming her way, 'All you need now is a big straw hat and you could be taken for one of the Riff women. Although, on second thoughts, I doubt it,' he inclined his head at her. 'Your skin's too fair, and that straight little nose is anything but Moorish.'

Her lips parted in fearful expectancy, Vivienne looked at him and beyond him to the departing hospital van, she asked, 'What is it? What's been happening? I've been so worried I didn't know what to think.'

Trent didn't reply at once. Beneath the weariness of his features she tried to glean something. Then he said, taking her arm, 'Let's find somewhere to sit, shall we?' She was wondering where she could deposit the fragrant contents of her arms when he added, 'No, keep the flowers. You make a soothing picture for a fellow who's been having something of a rough ride lately.'

He led her down the steps to a seat in a sunken garden area below the level of the croquet lawn at the side of the house. There was the early evening drone of insects here, and the slender boles of young lime trees were silvered against the paling blue sky. When they were seated Vivienne waited and Trent said, 'It was the X-ray thing that started it all off.'

'Started what?' Vivienne rested the flowers in her lap with an impatience that brought a glimmer of tolerant humour to Trent's blue gaze. He went on to explain, 'It seems that Rob's wrist is healing good and strong.'

Vivienne looked blank. Then she asked on a quick breath, 'Was that so entirely unexpected?'

'No,' Trent shook his head. 'Rob's trouble is muscular, but ...'

'But what?' Vivienne was acutely conscious just then of the evening song of a rock thrush in a nearby tree.

Trent shrugged. 'To the doctors it seems to have some sort of significance.' He waited, then went on almost casually, 'They want him to go to the hospital tomorrow for some tests.'

Vivienne's heart was thumping in a curious restrained way. Her wide amber gaze still clung to Trent's, the faint signs of wonder and hope there mirrored in his. For an immeasurable time they sat, neither saying a word, then Trent stirred himself and helping her as she mechanically scooped up the flowers he drawled, 'We'd better go in and see about getting changed, otherwise Momeen will be serving to an empty table tonight.'

The evening dragged for both of them, and the hours between dark and daylight were the longest that Vivienne had ever known. She rose early the next morning and putting on a cotton dress went down into the orchards. There was much activity, for the trees were becoming heavily laden and measures were being taken to protect the rapidly developing fruit. Watching the men operating the irrigation sluices, Vivienne saw along the road in the distance, the black limousine starting out on its journey into town. Abdul would be at the wheel, and Trent and Robert in the rear compartment. She turned quickly away and with her eyes over-bright she swung up a child, a toddler belonging to one of the workers. *She wouldn't let herself think, she wouldn't let herself hope too much.* If ever she needed to shut all thoughts of herself and Trent out of her mind, it was now.

The Berber women wore voluminous print dresses and hoods and shielded their faces shyly as Vivienne moved among them. She watched them up small step-ladders weeding out the inferior fruit, their children clambering about and constantly being cuffed into clearing up the ground beneath the trees of windfalls and unwanted growth. The puppy adopted by the estate workers and bearing the unlikely name of Panther was almost skinnily adult now and chased joyfully beneath the trees, leaping at birds and anything that moved.

The women had brought goat's cheese, dark bread and dates for their midday meal, and this they shyly asked

Vivienne to share. She sat with them in the shade of an old walnut tree, carefully averting her gaze from the road running through the orchards, yet every fibre of her being straining for the sound of a car engine.

The sun had slanted down across the bay and the men were making preparations for spraying the fruit trees when Vivienne's glance was momentarily dazzled by the flash of sun on gleaming metalwork. It was then that she saw the limousine slowly making its way back through the trees to the villa. The women were packing up ready to leave and with their children clinging to their skirts they wished her goodbye in their Berber tongue, and she returned their smiles and set off in the direction of the house. But her knees were weak and she found the walk back along the paths infinitely more nerve-racking than when she had started out that morning.

There was no sign of the car when she arrived on the terrace, so Abdul must have taken it straight round to the garage. She heard voices and saw by the open doors and windows that they came from the lovely ground floor room where she had been arranging flowers the previous afternoon. She moved in under the archways with a pulse hammering in her throat.

Trent was there, draped against the marble fireplace facing the doorway. And as she went in she saw Robert in his wheelchair beside the tapestry-covered sofa and the open windows. And when she looked at him she knew. With a hot and cold tingling of her senses, she knew. His flaxen hair was long and shaggy and adorable, hanging over the collar of his open-necked shirt. His blue eyes reflected the brilliance of the summer sky, though there was no sky visible at the moment, so that in itself was an indication if she hadn't already seen the slow grin forming on his lips at the sight of her.

The palpitating question must have been written all over her face, for he said, with a look at his brother, 'Tell her, Trent.'

Her glance swung to Trent's and not only was there that

same blueness there, but something else too, something warm and secretive and loving. He eased his frame into a new position beside the fireplace and spoke in that familiar lazy way of his, perhaps to disguise his emotions. 'What we were all hopeful of yesterday, but too scared to put into words, has been proved. Rob is on the way to being cured. According to his doctors, in a few weeks he'll be strong enough to leave his wheelchair, and in six months he'll be completely recovered.'

As Vivienne listened to the magic, *magic* words she felt her heart swelling till her head swam, and running across the room she opened her arms. 'Oh, Robert! I'm so happy for you!' She hugged him to hide the tears of joy in her eyes and straightened only when she had her emotions under control.

Robert smiled up at her, the excitement in him communicating itself in such a way that all three were powerfully aware of it. 'Do you know what this means, Viv?' There was that note of urgency in his tones, that earnest, ardent look in his eyes. 'It means we can get married.'

Vivienne felt herself falling, falling through black, imaginary space that made the room reel. Clutching for something, she threw a look at Trent and came up against the veiled shock in his face and in his eyes, then she heard herself saying with laughter that sounded harsh and grating in his ears, 'So we can!'

CHAPTER TEN

VIVIENNE listened to the jarring note of the rock thrush. There was no sweet sound coming from his throat as there had been the evening before. Though the trees cast their same sparkling green shade, jewelled by the slanting rays of the sun, this sunken garden that, twenty-four hours ago, had throbbed with life and hope was now a bleak and lonely place.

Haroun had taken Robert up to his room. Trent sat on the seat beside her. She said to him, continuing the conversation that had begun a few minutes ago, 'It's truly a miracle! Robert has been looking so ill, it made one imagine the worst.'

Trent nodded. 'I knew a little of what was going on. Some time back the doctors studying Rob's ailment found what they thought might be a breakthrough. They asked my permission to try out the treatment. They warned me that it might be rough on Rob and that there was no guarantee that anything would come of it.'

Listening to him clicked something in Vivienne's mind. 'That day before we drove to Tetuan—I remember now.' She turned to him. 'They kept you rather a long time at the hospital that morning.'

'That's right,' Trent affirmed. 'I didn't say anything then or later because I didn't want to raise anybody's hopes.'

Vivienne watched a butterfly spread its wings on a rock, making the most of the sun that was left, and somehow it reminded her of herself as she commented, 'The doctors must be feeling pleased with themselves.'

Trent nodded. 'There's no doubt that I'll be indebted to Paul Lazare and Georges Marne for life. I've dragged Rob round some pretty expensive clinics, but it took a couple of unknown specialists in a small-time hospital to do the trick.

174

It will be a difficult job, but I'll have to figure out some way of repaying them.'

'Have you got anything special in mind?' She had a feeling that they were both talking mechanically now.

'Well, I could donate some much needed equipment. Things like that . . .' Trent rose and took her arm and with this same feeling of inevitability they began to move indoors. Vivienne wondered, with a lump in her throat, if it was possible to be utterly and truly happy and heartbrokenly miserable at the same time. They had protected Robert from the truth. Now there was no way out, *ever*.

The croquet pitch had fallen into disuse. The physical exercise that Robert had indulged in in the past had been recommended to assist in the treatment, but now that he was going through the long recuperation period he had been ordered to rest. The sun had become blindingly hot beside the pool and for more than a week now they had spent the afternoons sitting beneath the shady vine awning at the side of the house, which looked on to the croquet lawn.

The grass was yellowing. Though it was watered daily it seemed to be losing its battle with the heat, and Vivienne, viewing it from her chair, likened her own condition to its fading glory. It seemed to her that she had ceased to live since that day when she had helped the Berber women in the orchards. She went through the motions, smiling, talking and being helpful where she could, but every now and again there were moments like now, when she looked at Trent lounging lazily nearby, yet tautly remote from her; when she knew that he was near enough to touch her but that he would never let himself. It was then that the ache inside her became almost too much to bear.

Robert was in his wheelchair a short distance from them, browsing through his volumes of poetry. He was happy and that was all that mattered. *But was it all that mattered? Didn't they have a life too?*

Robert was shaking his head. 'You'll never get it right,

Viv.' She had been trying to put some lilt into the verse he had rehearsed with ther. If only he knew how difficult it was for her! 'This is the way it should go.' He read the words out feelingly. '*I love thee with the passion put to use in my old griefs, and with my childhood faith*—— Now you.'

Vivienne took her cue, tight laughter in her throat. '*I love thee with a love I seemed to lose with my lost saints*——' she floundered, and then a voice at their backs finished,

'*I love thee with the breath, smiles, tears, of all my life— and, if God choose, I shall but love thee better after death.*'

A hush had settled over the afternoon. Those words spoken simply yet with an unselfconscious sincerity had an odd effect on all of them. Vivienne turned slowly, almost knowingly, then rising from her chair she exclaimed, 'Lucy!'

The small figure standing just outside the awning came forward. 'Hello, Viv, I heard your voice. I'm on holiday in Tangier for two weeks and I thought I'd look you up. I hope you don't mind?'

Vivienne was in a daze. *Lucy here!* She had let her hair grow long so that it fell in pale strands to her shoulders. She was wearing a stylish summer dress, and there was a glow about her. *It was the letter.* Of course, now Vivienne knew. The one she had written explaining that Robert wasn't going to die. Dear Lucy! Her happiness shone from her like a torch, giving her face a radiance that made it appear almost beautiful.

'Well, somebody get the girl a chair!' Robert stared fascinated at their guest as though still lost in those final spoken words of the poem. Vivienne jumped to the task. She daren't look at Trent, but she could feel him trying to catch her eye bemusedly. She made the introductions smiling away her nerves.

'This is Lucy Miles, a friend of mine from England. Lucy, meet Robert Colby. And this is his brother Trent.'

Trent, who had already risen to reach for a chair, came

forward and said with a lazy gleam, 'I'm very glad to know you, Lucy.' After which Robert butted in, barely giving her time to sit down,

'Hey, where did you learn to speak poetry like that? You must have read that piece a hundred times to be able to say it without fluffing a single syllable.'

'Well, I do know it rather well,' Lucy admitted, smiling. 'But it's easy really.' She opened her neat white handbag and took out a small leather-bound book. 'I've got all the Brownings' poems here and I just look at them whenever I feel like it.'

'Gosh!' Robert took the book from her and flicked through it, impressed. 'I've never seen anything like this.' He grinned wryly at the heavy volumes on the table beside him. 'That's the way I read poetry. I didn't know there were gems like this to make it so simple.'

'You can buy them,' Lucy nodded. She added shyly, 'If you like I'll make a present of it to you.'

'Goodness, I couldn't let you do that!' His blue gaze swung to meet her gentle grey one. Then he said with an eager smile, 'Or on second thoughts we could do a swop. I haven't got any pocket editions like this, but I have got a biography of the Brownings. And I'll tell you what else I've got—a real old copy of Browning's works. It's got his signature on the fly-leaf and it's all done in gold lettering on the cover. Trent said it must be pretty valuable.'

'I'd like to see it,' said Lucy. There was a shy eagerness in her too.

'You will.' Robert seemed aware of it. He stirred himself to exclaim, 'Hey, aren't we going to offer our guest any refreshment? Some tea or something like that.'

Vivienne jumped up. 'Certainly! I'll go and see to it myself.'

'Not the mint stuff, Viv,' Robert called after her. 'I bet Lucy would like real English tea.'

'That would be nice,' came the soft reply as Vivienne hurried off towards the side door into the house. Haroun was dozing just inside. Momeen was down in the Casbah with his wife and children and Maurice wouldn't arrive for some time yet, so she would have to cope on her own.

In the big airy kitchen she set out a tray with cups and saucers and filled a plate with thin bread and butter and another with some of Maurice's delicacies from the pantry. Eventually the kettle boiled and with the big silver teapot steaming at the spout she transferred the lot out of doors.

When she arrived back under the awning Lucy and Robert were engaged in a lighthearted argument. 'No, it was Elizabeth who first made her mark in English literature. Her husband's earlier poems were hard to understand and nobody took much interest.'

'Yes, but that was *before* they were married. Don't forget that Elizabeth Barrett was six years older than Browning. Recognition of his talent came slower, that's all.'

'True, but in their fifteen years of married life in Italy Elizabeth was very prolific.'

'Even so, today Browning is considered the greater poet of the two.'

Trent came to take the tray from Vivienne and this time his gaze met hers. It was quizzically enquiring. The bandying went on and she poured the tea and handed the cups around, and by the time the food on the plates had dwindled to nothing, demolished mainly by Robert, it had been agreed by the two gay participants in the discussion that Elizabeth Browning was now the lesser known poet of the two.

Vivienne stacked the cups and saucers on the tray and with her cheeks attractively flushed Lucy brushed the crumbs from her dress and rose to say shyly, 'Well, I ought to be going. I only arrived this morning, and I haven't unpacked yet.'

'What about the books?' Robert looked at her a little glowing-faced himself. 'The biography. And you can borrow the other one if you like. I'd get them for you if I wasn't kind of stuck here.' He tapped the arms of his wheelchair. 'Mind you, this thing is only temporary. In a few weeks I'll be saying goodbye to it for good.'

'I know where the books are,' Vivienne offered. 'And perhaps Lucy would like to come up to my room to freshen up before she goes?'

'A good idea,' Robert grinned.

Vivienne led the way indoors. Neither girl spoke as they went up the stairs, but once they were in the bedroom with the door closed behind them all pretence disappeared.

'Lucy!'

'Viv!'

They hugged each other, then drew apart to gaze laughingly at one another. Lucy was the first to put her thoughts into words. 'You've grown lovely, Viv. A little thinner perhaps, but you've lost that hard look.'

Vivienne smiled. 'And what about you?' She eyed the smart dress and pretty hair-style, exclaiming, 'Can this really be my friend Lucy Miles?'

Lucy looked happy. She said, 'Dad's been given some kind of government allowance to run the farm, so things aren't half as tight as they used to be at home. I only got your letter the day before yesterday. After I'd read it I went straight out and booked a holiday here.'

Vivienne's smile drooped a fraction. 'It hasn't been easy, being here with Robert.'

'He doesn't suspect at all, does he?' asked Lucy.

'Not at all,' Vivienne replied.

'It doesn't matter,' Lucy said simply. 'Nothing matters now that he's going to be all right.'

'Hey, girls!' Robert's voice came from below outside. 'What's taking you so long?'

They smiled at one another. Lucy spent a moment or two tidying up while Vivienne slipped upstairs to the left wing rooms for the books, then they went downstairs and out to the terrace together. Robert had wheeled himself round from the side of the house. Trent and Haroun were just appearing from that direction. Lucy had in her hands the gold-lettered volume. She said, fingering through it reverently, 'It's a beautiful book. Are you sure you want to trust it to me?'

'I've a feeling I could trust you with my life, Lucy,' Robert joked.

She smiled at him shyly and murmured, 'I promise to take great care of it.'

Vivienne was just on the point of asking her friend how she was going to get back to the hotel, when Lucy said hesitantly, 'I wonder if someone could make a phone call for me? I came up here in a taxi and ...'

'A taxi?' Robert turned in his wheelchair. 'We can't let you go back in a taxi. Can we, Trent?'

Trent shrugged his shoulders good-humouredly. 'Abdul's rubbing the Bentley up at the back. We can ask him to run it round here if you like.' He said something to Haroun and the big Moor went off at a trot.

While they were waiting Lucy looked along the drive and spoke softly. 'It's beautiful here. Those cedars must be really old.'

'We've got some even older ones out beyond the pool,' Robert said beside her. 'You can't see them from here, but they're the kind that make you want to sit down with a book.'

The limousine appeared and came to a stop at the front of the house. Abdul, dutifully impassive, stepped out and held the door open.

Lucy had taken her seat and the door was being closed when Robert said, 'Aren't you going to ask your friend to call again, Viv? She can come here any time she wants. That's okay, isn't it, Trent?'

'Sure. Any friend of Vivienne's is always welcome,' Trent replied with an idle grin.

Robert turned his eager glance back to the open window and added tentatively, 'That is, if you've got no other plans ... I mean ...'

Lucy gave him her shy smile. 'I'm here for a whole fortnight and I've got nothing special to do at all,' she said happily.

She waved as the car started out and the others waved back until it was out of sight round the bend of the drive, then they turned towards the house. Haroun was on hand to push the wheelchair up the ramp at the side of the marble steps and as they went in beneath the shady archways Robert said dreamily, half to himself, 'Can you imagine! She spoke those words of the poem almost as though they'd been made for her.'

'Imagine!' Trent echoed, a whimsical note in his voice.

Lucy came soon after lunch the next day. Robert had spruced himself up, and in white sports shirt and pale blue shorts he looked boyishly handsome. They sat for a little while beside the pool, but Robert was impatient for Lucy to see everything. 'I was going to show you those cedars. You see where those palms are? We can go this way.'

Vivienne rose. She was about to start pushing the wheelchair when Lucy said diffidently, 'May I try?'

'Of course,' Vivienne laughed. She thought for a moment and added, 'Actually I've got quite a few things to do in my room. I've neglected all kinds of jobs lately, so your being here will give me a chance to catch up a little.' She left them smilingly to it and made her way back to the house.

Her room had never gone through such a cataclysmic change. During the following days she cleaned out drawers, washed out smalls, polished mirrors and furniture and even gave the damask drapes over her bed an airing. And most afternoons Robert and Lucy's voices could be heard coming from the side of the pool, or they could be found sitting together beneath the old cedars, or wandering where the water splashed in the mosaic fountain near the palms, or examining the ancient foliage in the old grounds close to the *minzah*.

The shady vine area which looked on to the croquet lawns was deserted. Sometimes Vivienne and Trent would sit there alone gazing at the yachts and fishing boats in the blue bay. Once when they rose together to go indoors they almost brushed against each other. It would have been easy then to give way to the powerfully sweet magnetic force which threatened to draw them close.

Summer cast its warm veil over the countryside and the days were fragrant with the swelling fruit in the orchards. On the last afternoon of Lucy's holiday they were in the lovely reception room which looked out on to the shady archways. Robert had his wheelchair near the open doorway. Vivienne was sitting on the tapestry sofa stitching lace round a handkerchief. Trent had just come in.

Robert, keeping an ear open for footsteps along the drive, seemed fidgety and awkward and looked as though he wanted to speak. He said suddenly, in a rush, 'Viv ... I've been meaning to mention it to you. That day when I came back from the hospital. What I said was ... sort of in the crazy mood of the moment. A fellow doesn't want to rush things like ... well, you know ... like marriage and things like that ...'

'Of course not, Robert. I understand.' Vivienne went on stitching her handkerchief. She said after a moment, a smile twitching her lips, 'A lot of things have happened since then. There's been Lucy's arrival and ...'

'We've enjoyed having her here. What we've seen of her.' From his place near the fireplace Trent took up the conversation drily. 'Too bad this is Lucy's last afternoon.'

Robert coloured, then he said with a look of relief and a grin, curbing the excitement in his tones, 'It might not be. She thinks her father will let her extend her stay, then she wants me to go and see her home in Ayleshurst. She lives on a farm too. Can you beat that!'

'Small world!' Trent drawled, playing down the irony in his expression.

His ears tuned, Robert suddenly sat up. 'That's her.' And with barely a glance their way, 'Do you mind if I go?' He took the ramp down the outside steps at a giddy speed and on the drive he yelled, 'Hey, Lucy! Stay where you are. I'm coming out to you. Watch this for wheelchair manoeuvrability!'

A short while later the sound of voices and laughter came from somewhere in the distance then faded gradually in the grounds.

The silence in the room was magnified by the twitter of the birds outside, by the steady ticking of the china clock on the mantelpiece. Vivienne went on stitching at the lace, her temples throbbing with the effort of remaining still. In the end she had to lift her head and when she did Trent's gaze was there, as it must have been for some time, waiting to meet and hold with hers.

For a long moment they stayed this way, then, wavering depths in his voice, he said, 'Come here to me.'

Vivienne placed down her lacework obediently and rose, but she never remembered crossing the space. It was as though she was in Trent's arms the very next second and his lips were fastening fiercely but tenderly upon her own. To give at last after these weeks of torment, after being held so long apart, was like being released from some sort of hell. There was no controlling the intensity of this first carefree embrace; no staying the force of unleashed emotions. Nor would Vivienne have wanted to. It was Trent who raised his head at last and said with a shaky laugh, 'Let's sit down, shall we?'

With their arms around each other's waists they wandered over to the sofa. Vivienne sat with her head on Trent's shoulder. After a while he said with an expansive grin, his glance circling the room, 'How do you feel about living among French antiques?'

Vivienne smiled. 'It's a lovely house, but a little overpowering.'

Trent nodded. 'I bought it from a French diplomat. I threw in a few Moroccan pieces of art and thought that would do the trick, but I guess it needs a woman's touch.' He kissed her on the tip of her nose.

With his arm around her, Vivienne thought about it. 'We could thin out the furniture a little, add a few lighter pieces.'

'That should do it. And hold a few parties. The place needs to be livened up a bit. Besides, I want the whole of Tangier to meet my wife.' His lips found the lobe of her ear.

'We'll have to tell Robert.' She turned to look at him.

'I don't think it will come as much of a surprise to him,' Trent gleamed. 'The lad's got eyes in his head, and he's pretty shrewd.'

'But he doesn't know about the business of the letters and that I came here in another girl's place,' Vivienne pointed out.

Trent shrugged. 'He'll find out one day. When he does it won't mean anything. He loves Lucy and that's all that matters.'

'He's always loved Lucy, and she him. Which reminds me,' there was mischief in Vivienne's expression and that I-told-you-so note in her voice, 'a certain someone going by the name of Trent Colby is going to have to eat his words, I think. So there's no lasting relationship to be got out of letter writing, is there?'

Trent capitulated without a fight. 'I'm willing to admit anything with you in my arms.' He pulled her closer.

'Even that you plagued me unmercifully about the casino?' she flashed teasingly.

'Sure! I enjoyed getting your back up,' he grinned. 'It gave me a kind of mean satisfaction for what you were doing to me.'

'Oh! And what was I doing to you?' she asked innocently.

'Driving me slowly out of my mind.' His grip on her tightened. 'Do you know what I went through, watching you every day at the pool with Rob?'

'Something happened to us, didn't it, that day we went to Tetuan. I felt it too.' She traced the line of his jaw with her finger.

Trent's eyes on her darkened. 'It was hell for me knowing how it was with Rob then. I tried to shut you out of my thoughts, and out of my mind. But you were there, just a kiss away, each day. It was more than flesh and blood could stand.'

'I was lucky.' Vivienne smiled reminiscently. 'I was wrapped up in thoughts of Gary. I'd already convinced myself in those early days that you were an overbearing tyrant.'

'This Thornton guy?' Trent's eyes darkened in a different way. 'I don't mind mentioning now that, that night in my office when I thought there was something between you two, I could cheerfully have torn him apart. Tell me about him.'

'There's nothing much to tell,' Vivienne shrugged. 'I'd never meant anything to Gary. But I foolishly believed he meant something to me. I'm glad I met him again. It's cleared the air in that direction for good.'

'In that case I'm glad too.' Gently he dropped a kiss on her mouth.

Her head resting back on his shoulder, she said dreamily, 'I was thinking—we could have a double wedding.'

'Not on your life!' Trent's gaze glowered humorously above hers. 'Rob will have to wait several weeks before he's fit. I'm fit now.' He joined her in dreaming idly up at the ceiling. 'You can have Lucy for a bridesmaid and Rob can be my best man. How's that?'

'Perfect!' Vivienne breathed beside him.

After a moment he said, 'How do you fancy Tahad island for a honeymoon?'

'Just the two of us?' Vivienne smiled thoughtfully. 'I'm not sure my cooking will come up to Maurice's excellence.'

'I'll manage,' came the reply. 'There'll be other things to compensate.'

'Trent Colby!' Vivienne twinkled severely. 'How could you!'

'That's a leading question.' With a grin he took her in his arms.

After a long moment she asked, 'What will happen about the casino?'

'I'll get rid of it and find some other occupation. But we'll think about work and business later.'

As his lips explored her throat she said firmly, 'You'll need a job to expend your energies on.'

'Some of them,' he replied with a wicked glint. After which she twinkled scoldingly,

'I think it's time we took a walk!'

Arms about each other, they strolled out and down into the gardens beside the pool. And here, where the sounds of voices and laughter came from another part of the grounds, they wandered until the first pink clouds of evening cast a rose glow over the city below. From the top of the minarets, in the old town and the new, the muezzins began to call the faithful to prayer. And to Vivienne, standing there with singing heart, it was as though the whole world was proclaiming their love. Hers and Trent's.

Also available this month
Four titles in our Mills & Boon
Classics Series

*Specially chosen re-issues of the best in
Romantic Fiction*

October's Titles are:

THE HOUSE OF THE AMULET
by Margery Hilton

'Fear not the desert, nor the destiny you deny,' the sand-diviner told Melissa when she came to Morocco. But Melissa feared the dark arrogant Raoul Germont even more. And he was the only man who knew the truth behind her missing sister's disappearance ...

THE AUTUMN OF THE WITCH
by Anne Mather

To save her father from ruin, Stephanie had married Santino Venturo. He had made it clear that he had married her only because he wanted a companion for his small daughter — but why, oh, *why* had he done it at all?

THE ATLANTIC SKY
by Betty Beaty

'The Atlantic weather is harsh, unpredictable and sometimes immeasurably violent.' So was Captain Prentice of World-Span Airways. And Air Stewardess Patsy couldn't get him off her mind.

BELOVED BALLERINA
by Roberta Leigh

Lucie Marlow was a brilliant and dedicated ballet dancer — which might have become a problem when she married Julian Summerford. But the real danger that threatened Lucie's marriage was the overwhelming jealousy of her mother-in-law.

Mills & Boon Classics
— all that's great in Romantic Reading!

BUY THEM TODAY only 50p

DON'T MISS OCTOBER'S
GREAT DOCTOR - NURSE ROMANCES

NURSE IN DISGRACE *by Carol Hughes*
Forced to resign from her hospital nursing post
because of an alleged association with a married man,
Tammy found the only obtainable job for her was in a
holiday camp. The re-appearance of dashing Dr.
Nicholas van Eiden only just saved her from another
scandal.

SISTER PETERS IN AMSTERDAM *by Betty Neels*
Sister Peters was delighted to be chosen, under the
new exchange scheme, as the British representative to
work in an Amsterdam hospital. It proved an interesting new life in more ways than one, and she found
that emotional problems could be just as complicated
in Holland as ever they could be at home.

**LOOK OUT FOR THEM AT YOUR NEAREST
MILLS & BOON STOCKIST** Only 50p

Forthcoming Mills & Boon Romances

DAY OF POSSESSION *by Lilian Peake*
Drake Warrick seemed to have the worst possible opinion of
Ilona. How could she manage to persuade him that he was
wrong about her?

FULL CIRCLE *by Kay Thorpe*
Sara and Steve Masters had become reconciled after five years
of separation — but what if the wheel came full circle and yet
again they found themselves unable to live together?

MASTER OF FORRESTMEAD *by Anne Hampson*
What would happen to Jodi when the masterful Shaun
Wyndham regained his memory and discovered that his
affections were engaged elsewhere?

BELOVED BENEFACTOR *by Yvonne Whittal*
Toni knew she could love Tarquin Radloff — but why did he
persist in treating her as a child?

CAPTIVE DESTINY *by Anne Mather*
Jordan had come back into Emma's life, saying he loved her
still. But she was now married to someone else . . .

CASTLE OF TEMPTATION *by Flora Kidd*
Dominic Lietch's presence at Ardgour could only complicate
matters for Aline — he still had the power to hurt her as he
had all those years ago . . .

THE LONG SURRENDER *by Charlotte Lamb*
Ashley Dent had forced Selina to marry him again — but could
she ever overcome the fear that had ruined their marriage the
first time?

GREEN MOUNTAIN MAN *by Janet Dailey*
Bridget still hated Jonas for walking out on her ten years ago,
and he could not forgive her for marrying another man. Could
they ever become reconciled?

DESIGNING MAN *by Rachel Lindsay*
(Design for Murder by Rachel Lindsay)
Alex Smith was aware of the tension between Henri Duval and
his son Paul. Her involvement was to deepen when Henri was
murdered . . .

RETURN TO SILBERSEE *by Jane Arbor*
Juliet was reluctant to leave Silbersee, and when the overwhelming Karl Adler came storming into the place, she knew
she would have to stay and fight!

Available November 1978 — Only 50p each

Cut-out and post this page to order any of the
popular titles (overleaf) from the exciting NEW

Mills & Boon
Golden Treasury
COLLECTION

EXCLUSIVE, DIRECT-DELIVERY OFFER

BRAND NEW — **Exclusive** to regular Mills and Boon readers **only** on
DIRECT-DELIVERY ORDERS **by post!** This unique series brings you
the **pick** of our all-time, best-selling romances by top-favourite
authors . . . . . . all newly republished, in a thrilling new format,
as the MILLS AND BOON GOLDEN TREASURY COLLECTION.
See overleaf for details of the first 10 wonderful titles — all
available NOW at just 45p each! HURRY! Make **your** selection
NOW and place your **DIRECT-DELIVERY ORDER** below.

Post to: *MILLS AND BOON READER SERVICE,
P.O. Box 236, 14 Sanderstead Road, S. CROYDON,
CR2 0YG, England.
Please send me the titles I have ticked □ overleaf from
the NEW Mills and Boon Golden Treasury Collection.

I enclose £ . . . . (No C.O.D.).
Please add 8p postage and packing per book ordered.
(Maximum charge: 48p for 6 or more titles).
Please write in BLOCK LETTERS below

NAME (Mrs/Miss) . . . .

ADDRESS . . . .

CITY/TOWN . . . .

POSTAL/ZIP CODE . . . .

**South African and Rhodesian readers please write for
local prices to P.O. Box 11190, Johannesburg 2000, S. Africa.*
GT/1440

191

ORDER NOW FOR DIRECT DELIVERY